STO

Cassie's Village

CASSIE'S VILLAGE

FRANCES RIKER DUNCOMBE

Illustrated by W. T. Mars

Lothrop, Lee & Shepard Co., Inc.

NEW YORK

Library of Congress Catalog Card Number: 65-13391

Printed in the United States of America.

Contents

Foreword

Because so much of this book is true, I wish to point out a discrepancy in time. Ground for the new and larger Croton Dam was actually broken in September, 1892. For story purposes, historical events that took place between then and 1895 have been condensed into the space of one year.

None of the characters are real, but people very much like them did live in the old village of Katonah.

F.R.D.

Cassie's Village

1

Stranger on the Bridge

Cassie Bates put a fresh grasshopper on her hook and flicked it back into the river, where the current carried it downstream from the bridge on which she was standing. If it were free to travel like the yellow leaf drifting on the surface, it would float past the village, around the bend, then on to the millpond at Whitlockville and over the dam. It would leave the Cross River to enter the Croton and eventually it would reach the Hudson and be carried south to New York City.

Cassie knew the route it would take because Mr. Tyler, the school principal, had pointed it out on a map last year. Mr. Tyler had been to New York City often, but hardly any of the boys and girls in sixth grade had been farther than White Plains. Cassie herself hadn't been that far, though the railroad track ran right past Pa's blacksmith shop and the sound of the train was as familiar to her as the sound of Pa's hammer striking against a horseshoe on his anvil.

It would be nice to go to New York some day, Cassie thought when she thought about it at all. For the most part she didn't want to think about any place beyond a ten-mile radius because she was too happy to be where she was, living with Pa in the little red house next to the shop at the south end of the village of Katonah.

Cassie couldn't even remember her mother who had died when she was a baby, and until two years ago she hadn't seen much of Pa either. She had lived in turn with different aunts and uncles scattered throughout Connecticut. There were lots of aunts and uncles and dozens of cousins. Cassie liked most of them but just when she'd get to feel at home in one family and school, it would be some other aunt's turn to take her. Then the summer she was ten, Pa had driven up to Aunt Sadie's on her birthday and taken her back with him to live. Everyone had agreed that a ten-year-old girl was plenty old enough to housekeep for her pa.

That had been in June of 1892; now it was September of 1894. For the first time in her life Cassie had gone to the same school for more than a year and kept the same friends. Right now, while she fished, she was listening for two of them. Or rather for the creak of oarlocks and splash of oars that would tell her they were coming, while the willows leaning over the water still hid them from view. When Emma Ferris and Josie Miller finished their morning chores they were going to stop by for her on their way to the flats where the rushes grew.

The fishline jerked and the water rippled. Cassie forgot about Josie and Emma. From the feel she knew she had hooked another trout and until she had it safe out of the water she was too intent even to notice that she was no longer alone on the bridge.

"That's a beaut. Wish I had a pole."

Cassie looked up then to see a strange boy standing beside her. He was medium tall and medium thin and was wearing city-bought clothes. Cassie didn't bother to notice anything more about him because she wasn't much interested in boys.

"Use mine if you want. I only need two fish for supper anyway and I've got them." Skillfully she removed the hook from the trout and handed pole and grasshopper can to the stranger.

Once his line was in the water he seemed to forget about it.

"You live around here?"

"Over there." Cassie pointed to the blacksmith shop and house behind it.

"What's that thing on top that looks like a cross?" he wanted to know.

It *was* a cross, put on the roof of the shop years ago when there had been talk of condemning land to make a reservoir. That was before Cassie had come to Katonah to live but people had told her the crosspiece on the pole was supposed to mark the expected water level. Nothing had come of it, though, and mostly she forgot the cross was there.

She was about to explain all this when a long-drawn-out *"Cassee-ee"* floated up the river and a flat-bottom boat pushed through the overhanging willow branches. Josie's red pigtails and Emma's blond curls were close together as the girls each pulled on an oar.

Cassie shouted back and then turned again to the boy. "I've got to leave now," she told him. "Would you mind taking my fish and the pole to the shop when you are through? Pa will take care of them." She picked up a string bag filled with apples that was lying beside her fish.

"Sure thing. My father's there now. I'm waiting for him to finish his business."

So his father had business with Pa! What sort of business would bring a city man all the way to Katonah to see Pa? Just one sort in Cassie's experience. A frown, half worry, half anger, drew her brows together.

"Your pa is one of those city patent lawyers." It was an accusation, not a question. All the friendliness had disappeared from her voice. Patent lawyers just seemed to smell it out when Pa had a new invention; then everything he had put by went into their pockets. Right now there was money in the dark blue sugar bowl but it rightfully belonged to Mr. Meech, their landlord. Tomorrow was rent day.

"Casseee-eee." The boat was halfway between bend and bridge. Cassie glanced toward her friends and then toward the blacksmith shop, unable to make up her mind. Supposing she went back and reminded Pa that he'd promised not to spend anything more on patents for a while? No, it would be no use. He'd promised before but he just couldn't seem to keep from doing it. Hot tears of anger came to her eyes as she faced the boy and she stamped her foot so hard that the loose boards of the bridge rattled.

"Listen, you just take that patent lawyer pa of yours and git, and don't you ever come here again!"

The boy looked at her in amazement, as though unable to believe the little dark-eyed, dark-haired girl who had seemed so friendly could have turned into this small fury.

"What you got against lawyers? Anyway my father isn't one, so there's no cause to fly off the handle. He's an engineer and I'm going to be one, too, when I grow up. Want to get mad some more about that?"

For a moment they stared at each other belligerently and then Cassie burst out laughing. An engineer! A man who drove a train! She sure had been a long way off in her guess. She gave the boy a rueful smile.

"Pa calls me a spitfire and I guess I am. Sorry I let out at you like that."

"Forget it," he replied. "You just surprised me, that's all."

In another minute the boat reached them and Cassie dropped into it as it passed beneath the bridge.

Pretty blue-eyed Emma and Josie, a green-eyed skinny little tomboy, were Cassie's very best friends and the three girls were almost constantly together. In the summer time it was generally on the river.

"I thought we'd never get here," Emma complained, giving up her seat to Cassie and moving to the one in the bow. "Just as we were leaving, Mama asked me to take a pie to that horrid old Mrs. Blaney." Emma's father was the Presbyterian minister and her mother always baked extra pies for the poor of the parish.

"It was worth being late." Josie giggled and held up a red-checked napkin, tied at the corners. "Look, doughnuts! We met Aunt Hattie Dickinson on the way and she gave us these."

Emma was gazing dreamily back at the bridge as the oars took the boat upstream. "Who's that boy, Cassie? I never saw him around before. He's real handsome; almost as handsome as Alfred Meech." Emma was thirteen, a year older than the other two and she was always noticing boys.

Josie took a large bite out of a doughnut and examined the boy critically as the space widened between them. "Summer boarders wear clothes like his sometimes, but it's too late for summer boarders now. They've all gone back to the city."

"Says his pa's an engineer." Cassie didn't really care who the boy was or what his father did, just so long as he wasn't going to take Pa's money for patents. But she couldn't say this, even to Emma and Josie, her best friends. Loyalty to Pa prevented.

Pa had taken out patents on a jack and a monkey wrench and a new kind of springs for carriages. Then there was the thing he called a tire-upsetter for use in tightening rims on wheels. They all worked fine and on each he'd thought to make a fortune, but it hadn't happened that way. The only money made was by the patent office and the lawyers. Now he'd invented some new improvement for a capstan, a sort of windlass on a vertical base, and it was this that Cassie had feared he was about to spend more money patenting.

The river was fairly deep near the village because it was backed up from the mill dam, but the farther the girls rowed, the shallower it became. About half a mile from the bridge another river—really just a stream—entered it. Cassie and Josie sent the boat into this stream with a few quick hard strokes and then stood up to pole.

After a little, the boat scraped bottom. The girls threw a flatiron out to keep it from drifting and waded ashore where they followed the narrow river still farther upstream. Very little grew beyond this point except the rushes along the water's edge. There were no planted or pastured fields and the sandy earth showed between sparse browning grass. As far as they could see in any direction there was not a barn or a house. In the summer these treeless flats, extending to the railroad tracks, were almost unbearably hot, but now with the first hint of autumn the air was fresh as it passed over the level ground.

First the girls gathered the slim rushes which would later be cut in short lengths and tied in the middle to make scrub brushes; then they sat down to enjoy the lunch they had carried with them from the boat.

"Only two more days till school!" Josie made a face as she opened the package of cheese and bread and dill pickles she had brought from her father's market. "I do wish Pa and Ma wouldn't make me go. I could be real useful driving Old Bess around delivering orders, and have a lot more fun."

"You don't mean that!" Emma said in shocked tones. "Why, I just don't know what I'll do when I finish eighth grade next spring."

"I'm glad I have *two* more years." Cassie bit into a juicy red-cheeked apple. "This is the nicest school I've ever been to, and Katonah is the nicest place I've ever lived. I'm glad I can stay here forever."

Josie tossed a pickle at each of them and wrinkled her short freckled nose in disgust. "Teacher's pets, both of you," she teased, "and Emma is getting young-lady airs as well. Pretty soon she'll be too dignified to play hide-and-seek or tag. She'll let her skirts down and maybe even let boys kiss her."

Emma flushed scarlet and rose quickly to her feet. "I will, will I? Well, anyway, neither of you are fast enough to catch me *yet.* So there!"

She was off down the flats, skirts flying and hair streaming back from her slender graceful neck. The others followed but they couldn't catch her. No one could run as fast as Emma, and not even tomboy Josie could think up a dare she wouldn't accept.

At the end of the afternoon all three girls were tired and happy as they piled their rushes into the boat and started home. Once they reached the Cross River, the current carried them, almost without use of oars.

"I wonder what that boy was like." At the risk of

being teased again, Emma couldn't help wondering out loud as the bridge came into sight.

Cassie had forgotten him entirely but now an uneasy little feeling came over her. Had he really been telling the truth? Or had he just been making it up, about his father being an engineer, because she'd lit out so at patent lawyers?

When the boat came to the bridge, she climbed out quickly, eager to be home.

"See you tonight for hide-and-seek?" Josie asked, handing her a share of the rushes.

"See you," Cassie called back, already starting to run. Why would a railroad man have business with Pa, she asked herself now. She shouldn't have believed the boy.

No one was in the house when she reached it and she went at once to the blue sugar bowl and raised the lid. Drawing the money out, she counted it. All there. With a sigh of relief she put it back and replaced the lid.

Feeling a rush of gratitude, she decided to make Pa something special for supper. Fish and what else? A pie maybe. Taking a scoopful of flour from the bin, she put it in a bowl and carried it over to the kitchen table. Then she saw the note and decided against the pie. Pa wasn't going to be home. He had gone to shoe some horses at the trotting stables just across the Croton River and after that there was a meeting at the G.A.R. Hall.

Cassie didn't bother to make supper for herself; instead she had a bowl of bread and milk and honey. Then she tied little bundles of rushes together until it was time for the game of hide-and-seek that went on every summer evening till the whistle of the milk train sounded its curfew.

2

Crosspiece on the Pole

The main part of the village was called the "Triangle" because that is what it was. Railroad Avenue, on the east, ran along the tracks; Main Street led west to the Cross River; and the two were connected by River Street, which extended beyond the Triangle and followed the river's burbling course to Whitlockville. Technically all the Triangle was in bounds for hide-and-seek but generally the game kept close to the depot.

As Cassie ran up Railroad Avenue, milk cans were clattering and clanking on the loading platform and children were scrambling down over the sides of farm wagons even before the horses were brought to a halt. For the young of the outlying farms, as well as their parents, the trip to Katonah with milk to be shipped on the evening train was a social outing. They didn't want to miss one minute of playtime with their friends. Some were already clustered around the flagpole at the corner of Railroad and Main when Cassie joined the group.

Joe Daniels, a village boy whose father owned the printing office and newspaper, had begun counting out. "Ibbety bibbety sibbety sab, ibbety bibbety canal boat. O-U-T spells out!"

One by one the children were counted out until only Cassie was left.

"Cassie's it, Cassie's it," they chanted. "What will you give us, Cassie?"

"A hundred by fives." She closed her eyes and leaned her forehead against the pole which served as home base. "Five, ten, fifteen, twenty . . ." Feet scurried away in all directions, shoes sounding on wooden steps, pebbles striking against trees and lampposts.

"Twenty-five, thirty, thirty-five, forty, forty-five, fifty . . ." Cassie continued to count out loud, though it was probable no one was still near enough to hear her. Yes, there was, too. A wagon had just driven up and unseen feet passed the flagpole and rushed on in frantic haste to be hidden before Cassie finished.

"Fifty-five, sixty, sixty-five, seventy, seventy-five, eighty . . ." All was quiet now except for grown-up voices at the platform.

"Load my cans for me, will you, Cy? I want to go to the meeting." That was Mr. Armstrong from Mt. Holly, and the answering voice, "Be glad to, Jonah," belonged

to Cyrus Smith, the depot master.

"Eighty-five, ninety, ninety-five, a hundred. Ready or not, I'm coming!" Cassie shouted, opening her eyes and turning around. She looked south down Railroad Avenue and then west down Main Street. There, in the fast deepening dusk she thought she glimpsed a moving patch of white, back of the house in which Josie lived above her father's market. Throwing an occasional wary glance behind her to make sure no one was stealing home free,

Cassie hurried toward it. The patch moved, but to the right a stealthy footfall told her that someone was about to dash for safety. She stood still and listened, then as the footsteps broke into a run, she followed.

"Home safe—home safe! You're a slowpoke!" a tall fifteen-year-old boy with dark arrogant eyes taunted Cassie as she reached the flagpole a split second later. Then in lower tones he asked, "Seen Emma tonight?"

"No, I haven't." Cassie ran back to Main Street. She hadn't seen Emma, but even if she had, she wouldn't have told Alfred Meech. She didn't like the bold way he looked at Emma. It made her feel uncomfortable.

The white patch turned out to be a shirt hanging on Mrs. Miller's clothesline, but soon afterward Cassie caught Joe Daniels hiding behind some nail kegs on the porch of Hoyt Brothers' feed and hardware store and the game began all over again.

"I'll give you a hundred by twos," Joe said when everyone had gathered around the pole once more. That was lots of time. Joe always gave enough time to pick a good hiding place. Running down Railroad Avenue, Cassie tried to decide between the lilac bush next to the post office and the space under the barber shop steps. Then, outside the G.A.R. Hall, she stopped. The rain barrel! She reached in and found it only slightly damp at the bottom. Still hesitating, she heard Joe's "Ready or not I'm coming!" and made up her mind. Crouching in the empty barrel, knees up to chin, she heard Joe come down the street and held her breath. He passed near but didn't stop; then he turned back toward the flagpole. Cassie's heart had been knocking so hard that she was surprised Joe hadn't noticed it. Then, as it quieted, she heard voices above her head, coming from an open window in the Hall.

At first she didn't pay much attention because she was thinking about Emma and Alfred. Alfred's father owned the blacksmith shop and the house Cassie lived in. He owned buildings all over the village and held mortgages on more. Besides all this he owned the optical lens factory, the livery stable and most of the insurance company. Mr. Meech was the richest man in Katonah, but that didn't give his son the right to be so bossy and conceited. Emma couldn't really like Alfred—of course she couldn't—but why didn't she slap him when he looked at her the way he did?

Cassie was trying to decide about this when a voice from the meeting in the Hall cut into her thoughts.

". . . and so, gentlemen, in a matter of weeks ground will be broken for the new Croton Dam which has become necessary to insure New York City a larger supply of water. It will be ten miles from here; three miles below the smaller dam it replaces."

Cassie heard a chair scrape on the floor as it was pushed back. "How high will the new dam raise the water level here in Katonah?" It was Mr. Daniels, Joe's father, who asked.

"I can't answer that, sir; not until surveys have been made."

Cassie didn't recognize the voice but the words made her feel uneasy. Water level? Katonah?

The voice went on. "I have taken rooms for my family and myself at the Dickinson House, where I shall be at your service at all times."

"At our service!" Mr. Meech sneered sarcastically. "And what about my factory? It's right on the Cross River where it runs into the Croton. If your new dam backs water up that far, it will wipe me out. Well, let me tell *you,* you won't get away with it. I have friends high up with influence."

Other voices joined in and the gavel banged for order. Then Judge Donaldson spoke. "Gentlemen, let me remind you that Mr. Creighton is not responsible for New York City's demand for more water. May I suggest that we treat him with more courtesy?"

Cassie's head whirled and her stomach flopped. She felt sick all over. If a dam ten miles away could endanger the lens factory, then—then— She didn't want to listen any more, maybe getting all mixed up. She wanted Pa to explain.

Climbing out of the barrel she didn't rejoin the hide-and-seek game. She felt too upset. She ran home and sat hunched in the big wing chair that had belonged to Ma.

The whistle of the milk train blew and then a minute later its wheels clicked over the rails in back of the house. At last she heard Pa outside.

She flung herself at him as he entered. "Pa, tell me— I was in the rain barrel—I heard that strange man, and what Mr. Meech said. What does it mean, Pa?"

"Why Cassie, child, you're as cold as ice. To bed with you. There's nothing to worry about." Pa's voice was natural enough but his light blue eyes seemed darker the way they always did when he was worrying. He gathered her close and his blond beard tickled her forehead.

"But Pa, they talked about the water level. Isn't that what the crosspiece on the pole above the shop is supposed to show?"

"*Was,* Cassie. Probably the new surveys will show a much lower level. May not affect the village at all."

"Did the man say that, Pa?" Cassie wouldn't be put off.

"Well no, he didn't, honey. But he didn't say it *would*

make a difference, either. Mr. Creighton—he's the man from the Aqueduct Commission—said there's no way of telling how far the Croton water will back up into our river until new surveys are made."

"But if the new level is higher? What then, Pa?"

"Well, honey, we can always move on and rent in some other village. It ain't as though we owned."

"Oh, Pa!" Cassie wailed. "I don't *want* to move on! Not ever again. I want to stay right here forever, even—even if it's under water."

"You really feel that way, honey?" Pa's arm grew even tighter about her. "I thought just you and me being together was enough. That we could make out anywhere."

"You're the most important part of my being happy here," Cassie told him, "but besides, there's Emma and Josie and school and church and picnics and hide-and-seek and skating in winter and—and—oh, can't you *see,* Pa? I belong here!"

Pa sighed heavily as he dropped his arm and turned to look out of the window. "Well then, I guess we will just have to hope the water won't back up this far. Anyway there's no sense in borrowing trouble."

Cassie stayed awake worrying most of the night, but when she went to the post office the next morning, she met Josie who seemed without a care in the world.

"What happened to you last night?" Josie asked. "We looked and looked for you long after Joe caught me. We looked until the milk train came through."

"Oh, Josie, didn't you hear?" Cassie cried. "They're going to build a big new dam and the village may be flooded. Isn't it just awful?"

"Oh, that." Josie replied unconcernedly. "No sense worrying about it. Pa isn't worried. He says it won't happen. Come on, Cass, stop glooming. I have something really important to tell you. Alfred is as mad as a wet hen. You know why Emma wasn't in the game last night? Her mother had that Mr. Creighton's wife and son to supper and she needed Emma to help. And you know who the son is? He's the boy you loaned your fishing pole to—the one on the bridge that Emma thought was so handsome."

Suddenly she turned a handspring, red braids flying around her head like a pinwheel. "Goodness, Cassie, aren't you glad that boys don't even look at us? Let's go up in the woods and jiggle on the Rocking Stone till it makes real loud booms!"

Leaving the mail till later, Cassie went along with Josie. Halfway down Main Street they turned north, taking a path that ran through the woods back of the school and the Presbyterian manse and the Dickinson

House. There, on a hillside behind a tangle of vines already turning scarlet, was a large rock balanced on a smaller one like a giant teeter-totter.

Josie leaped on the flat surface of the large rock and one end came down, hitting the stony ledge beneath with a hollow boom that sounded a little like thunder. According to legend the rock had been used by Indians to send signals in the days of Chief Katonah and his followers.

When Cassie mounted it, too, the other end came down with an equally satisfying boom. After five minutes or so Emma appeared.

"You might have stopped by," she said aggrieved. "If I hadn't heard the stone, I might have wasted the whole morning looking for you."

"Thought you'd be with that boy. Thought you'd be too grown up now." Josie tossed her head.

"That's silly and you know it! Anyway, I'll always love playing here, even when I am grown up."

Cassie moved over to let Emma join them, and as the woods resounded with the soul-satisfying booms of the Rocking Stone, her fears began to fade.

"Ma used to do this, and so did her ma," said Josie, jumping down at last. "I guess my children will, too— that is, if I decide to have children instead of being a lion tamer."

"Oh, Josie, how can you even think of being a lion

tamer!" Emma exclaimed in disapproval. "Tightrope walking is so much more glorious!"

Ever since early summer when Stone and Van Amburgh's circus had given its yearly performance on the flats below Katonah, Emma and Josie had talked of joining it. Josie's loyalty had wavered between bareback rider and lion tamer, but Emma had remained true to tightrope-walking. She had practiced by laying clothesline on the grass and, later, by walking the board fence in back of the drugstore. She was better even than Alfred Meech, who was the only other person in all Katonah who could walk the fence. Now, as the girls returned to the village by way of the tracks, she stepped up on a rail and, placing one foot before the other with perfect balance and confidence, walked the entire distance without slipping once.

Cassie was just as fascinated by the circus as the other two, but even when she talked of joining it also, she knew she was just pretending. Traveling around the country, no week in the same place all summer long, was not what she wanted at all. What Cassie wanted was to stay in Katonah forever.

Suddenly fear returned. Maybe Pa and Josie were wrong. Maybe there wouldn't be a Katonah.

"Emma!" she called sharply, "what did they say—those Creightons, I mean—when they were having supper with you?"

"Well," Emma paused, one foot in the air and arms outspread for balance, "Ralph said he'd be starting school here on Monday, and Mrs. Creighton said her husband had asked your father to repair some tripods for surveying."

"I don't mean that sort of thing. I mean about the new dam and the water level."

"They didn't say anything about it. At least not while I was around. Gracious me, Cassie, there's no sense in getting excited. When Papa came home from the meeting, *he* said he didn't believe the new dam would make much difference anyway. Likely only the buildings right on the water would have to go, if any." She waved an airy hand. "Bye now. I promised Mama to try on some school dresses for her to let down."

Cassie's heart gathered in a tight, cramplike knot as she watched Emma leave. Emma hadn't meant to hurt; Cassie knew that. She had just repeated her father's words without thinking. *Only the buildings right on the water.* So the buildings farther back would be safe no matter what happened. But that needn't be true of the blacksmith shop and the house she and Pa lived in. They were on the water all right. From the porch of the little red house she could throw a stone and hear it plop into the river, and the shop next to it was about the same distance.

How could Emma have forgotten that? And Josie, too?

Hiding her hurt, Cassie left Josie a little farther on and stopped at the post office. The post office was in Arnold's Shoe Shop and Mr. Arnold was busy with a customer.

"Guess these copper-toed ones are what you'll be wanting. All the boys hereabouts wear 'em." He looked up and saw Cassie. "Want you to meet Ralph Creighton, Cassie. He'll be going to school with you this winter."

Ralph gave Cassie a friendly grin, but as she faced him all the fear and hurt she'd been holding back burst out in angry words.

"You should have told me—you should have told me your pa came here to drown Katonah. You didn't have to lie about his job!"

The next instant she turned and ran from the shop.

"Wait now, Cassie," she heard Mr. Arnold call, but she didn't stop running until she reached home.

3

The Dare

The next time Cassie saw Ralph was on the way to church, Sunday morning. Both the Methodist and Presbyterian churches were across the river from the Triangle, and skipping along to keep up with Pa's long strides, she saw the Creightons ahead of them on the bridge. Too far ahead, luckily, for Pa to greet them and expect her to speak politely to Ralph.

Cassie crossed her fingers behind her back. "I hope they'll be Methodists," she wished but her wish didn't come true. Half way up the street on the other side of the bridge, she saw them join Mrs. Ferris and Emma and enter the Presbyterian church under Alfred's baleful glare. For once Cassie was on Alfred's side. If she hadn't been afraid that Pa would catch her making faces, she would have glared too.

A few minutes later, though, rising for the first hymn, she forgot all about Ralph and how he'd lied to her.

Cassie loved church and most of all she loved the hymn singing. As she stood beside Pa, her voice rose clear and sweet from a heart in which there was no room for resentment. Then during the sermon, when her attention was apt to wander and she might have thought about Ralph again, she had something more important to think about. Just before the sermon Mr. Ferris always read the notices he'd been asked to announce from the pulpit. The first one was about the oyster supper that the Ladies' Aid was holding to reduce the mortgage on the manse. Tickets would be fifty cents.

"Want to go to it, honey?" Pa asked in a whisper.

Cassie nodded but before she could whisper back, Mr. Ferris began reading the second notice, the one that put everything else right out of her mind.

"The Planting Committee of the Village Improvement Society asks me to announce that twenty young trees will be set out at the south end of the Triangle on Saturday afternoon. Anyone wishing to assist can speak to Mr. Fowler after the service."

Twenty young trees at the south end of the Triangle? Why, that would be right on the water by their house and the shop. Planting there now must mean people thought it was safe; that the land wouldn't be flooded! Cassie's hopes zoomed upward and then spiraled down. Perhaps though, the notice had been written wrong? Perhaps it was meant to read the *east* end, which was two blocks back from the river?

She looked around to see if Pa or anyone else sensed a mistake. If anyone did she couldn't tell and Pa said "Shh" when she tried to ask. By this time the sermon had started and everyone was gazing straight ahead. Even Josie's eight-year-old twin brothers, Seth and Moses, who had a live frog on the seat between them just in front of Cassie, looked straight ahead while their hands were busy keeping the frog from escape and parental discovery.

All through the sermon Cassie fidgeted. She just had to know whether the notice was right or wrong. Then at last it was over. Mr. Ferris pronounced the benediction and the organ wheezed the first bars of the closing hymn.

Outside the church Cassie hurried over to the group on the lawn which included Mr. Fowler, the man in charge of the planting.

"Mr. Fowler, please, sir, is it the *east* end of the Triangle where the trees are to be planted?"

"Why, no, Cassie, the south end on River Street." He looked at her kindly. "Is your father aiming to help set them out?"

"I—I don't know. But Mr. Fowler, when the dam is built, won't the water cover the trees maybe?"

The other men had stopped talking and for a minute

Mr. Fowler didn't speak either. Then he waved toward the two good-sized evergreens that stood, one on each side of the wooden church. Like its own slim spire, they pointed straight up to heaven.

"You see those trees, Cassie? We planted them in 1875, the year the Water Commission sent up their first surveyors. We've planted every time they've sent men since. Not a tree has gotten wet feet yet."

It wasn't exactly an answer but it was enough to send Cassie's heart skyward. If the Planting Committee wasn't worrying, she didn't have to either. "I'll help you plant if you'll let me," she offered.

The men went back to their talk and Josie came up, her eyes and manner clearly indicating that she had news. She pulled at Cassie's arm.

"Behind the horse-shed," she whispered. "Alfred and Ralph Creighton. I think there is going to be a fight. We don't want to miss it!"

Behind the shed, Joe Daniels, Ollie Arnold, George Tyler, the school principal's son, and several other boys were watching what obviously they all hoped would develop into a fight. Alfred, at least ten pounds heavier and a year older than Ralph, was trying to make it one.

"So you're scared to fight me," he sneered.

"What's happened?" Josie asked eagerly.

Without taking his eyes from the two boys who faced each other, Joe replied, "Alfred told Ralph to stay away from Emma."

"And what did Ralph say?"

"Keep quiet, Josie. Listen."

"No, I'm not scared. It's just that I hardly know Emma." Ralph's voice was steady. "I won't say I'll stay away from her or any of the other girls till I get to know them, but it doesn't make sense to fight about it."

"You're yellow."

"It's like I said."

"Alfred," Mr. Meech called impatiently from the other side of the shed. "I am ready to leave. Where are you?"

"Coming, Pa." With a last contemptuous glance Alfred turned away from Ralph and walked off. The other boys followed. Ralph stared at their retreating backs without moving or attempting to speak; then he, too, left.

"Oh, Cassie, he shouldn't have refused to fight!" Josie cried. "Now none of the other boys will have anything to do with him."

"It will serve him right." Cassie's cheeks were hot and her dark eyes snapped. "I can't abide Alfred, but I was hoping he'd trounce Ralph good. It would even up for what he did to me—borrowing my fishing pole and lying about what his pa did for a living."

"Lying? About him being an aqueduct engineer?" Josie gave her a perplexed frown. "But Cassie, Ralph *did* tell you his pa was an engineer. You told Emma and me that, two days ago in the boat."

The angry flush died away from Cassie's face. She looked startled and then chagrined.

"Why, Josie, so he did! I guess I just *thought* he meant an engineer on a train. Oh dear, I shouldn't have flown out and accused him of lying yesterday. I suppose now I'll have to say I'm sorry. What a bother. Do you suppose I'll *ever* learn to hold my temper?"

Josie shook her head. "Guess not. But about Emma. Alfred's not going to let up on Ralph. He'll think of something else. You wait and see."

The next morning, for the first time in nearly three months, the strident peal of the school bell sounded again. The weather was still hot and Cassie's high button shoes scuffed up dust as she ran north up River Street, but it seemed cooler. It always seemed as if winter was about to begin once school started, even though it might be warm and stuffy inside the little two-room building on Palmer Avenue that smelled of yellow soap and chalk. Cassie loved the smell; she could hardly wait to take her first long sniff of it and to throw open the lid of the double desk she would share with some other girl.

Mr. Tyler and Miss Williams, who taught the lower grades, were standing on the porch welcoming the pupils as they arrived. Mr. Tyler was a strict-looking man with keen gray eyes behind thick glasses and a black handlebar mustache. Miss Williams was young and had a round, smiling face beneath a shining golden pompadour.

Once inside the door, the younger children filed into Miss Williams' room at the right of the hall and the older ones into Mr. Tyler's room at the left. When seats were assigned, Cassie found herself next to Josie again. Emma shared a desk with Estelle Whitlock on the opposite side of the room with the other eighth grade pupils. Directly behind Emma sat Ralph Creighton.

"Alfred's not going to like that one bit," Josie whispered behind the raised lid of the desk, and then she turned around to glare at the boy behind *her.* "Ollie Arnold, if you dip my braid in your inkwell even *once,* I'm going to paint your face with it!"

"Why honest—cross my heart—you know I wouldn't." Ollie smiled innocently and Cassie grinned. School, as it had been last year and the year before that, was again a fact.

The younger children had recess early. When it came time for the older ones, the girls, as usual, gathered at one end of the yard, and the boys at the other. There was no rule, even among themselves, that this must be, but it was accepted custom. Now, however, Cassie broke it. "I'll have to tell Ralph I'm sorry, sometime, so I may as well get it over with."

Josie nodded. "I guess so," she agreed.

Ralph, sitting alone on a rock apart from the other boys, received Cassie's rather grudging apology almost as though he weren't listening. His eyes were on the roof of the building and Cassie looked up too. Along the ridge Alfred Meech was inching his way to the girls' side.

Show-off, Cassie thought. Wants to show Emma how smart he is. Hope she isn't looking.

But Emma was looking. Not more than a minute after Alfred had swung himself to the ground on the girls' side by means of a maple branch, Emma appeared on the roof. No careful inching across for her. With arms outstretched she moved along the ridge like a dancer, never looking down, never wavering. On her face was the look of one who is experiencing ecstacy.

Cassie held her breath, as though even that small movement of air might unbalance her friend, but she need not have feared. Emma walked the ridge once; turned and walked it back; then rose on her toes and blew kisses from both hands like a professional performer accepting applause.

There was no applause in the usual sense; to have clapped or cheered might have brought one of the

teachers out of the building to investigate. But the admiration on every upturned face was as great as that evoked by the tightrope artist of Stone and Van Amburgh's circus. When Emma shinnied down the maple, Alfred sauntered up to Ralph.

"Now it's your turn. I dare you."

Ralph's face whitened. "I never walked a roof."

"Take the dare back, Alfred!" Cassie entreated. Her apology hadn't left her feeling any more friendly toward Ralph but she didn't want to see him killed. Alfred paid no more attention to her than to the buzzing of a fly.

"If even *girls* can walk it, you can't refuse without admitting you're yellow, city boy." The taunt was spoken softly; the sneer in the voice not to be borne.

"Don't Ralph," Cassie begged. "It's not a fair dare because no one in Katonah except Alfred and Emma could possibly do it. And they've been practicing on fences steady." She looked desperately across the yard to where the other boys stood watching. She knew they couldn't have heard; Joe at least would have had the fairness to object. "None of the other boys would take a one-sided dare like that. Joe will tell you—"

"No. Keep out of this." Slowly and deliberately Ralph stood up. "None of the other boys would *need* to take it."

He climbed an oak beside the roof easily enough but it was evident from his first step along the ridge that he would never make the other end in safety.

"Alfred, you shouldn't have! He'll be killed!" Cassie accused furiously and then hissed, "Shut up," as he started to speak. No one said a word from then on.

The boy on the roof, grim-faced and tense, swayed precariously, regained balance, took another step. Again he swayed and then went forward with a few running steps that he could neither continue nor slow. When his right foot slipped and his body arched backward, everyone knew there would be no recovery.

He fell. Rolling down the roof's slippery shingles, he hit first the wooden gutter and then, with a thud, the ground. After that he didn't move.

It was George Tyler who first broke the paralysis that held them all. He ran up the schoolhouse steps to fetch his father, the clatter of his boots sounding as loud as thunderclaps in the dreadful silence. Then Cassie found her own legs worked and she raced for Dr. Weare's house.

"Please, God, let him be in," she prayed on the run. "Or if that's too much to ask, let Mrs. Doctor be there. Please, God, let one of them be in."

4

Cassie Finds a Job

Mrs. Doctor Weare had only just arrived home and her black bag still lay on the table in her big sunny kitchen. She was sipping a cup of tea when Cassie dashed into the house without stopping to knock.

"Doctor, doctor, come quick!"

Mrs. Doctor, a short heavy-set woman with ruddy cheeks and near-white hair, sighed as she rose. She had been up all night helping the Proutys' sixth little baby into the world and she'd been counting on a nap.

"Doctor's not in, Cassie. What's wrong?"

"The new boy fell off the schoolhouse roof. I think he's dead—he hasn't moved."

"Probably wind knocked out. Boys have fallen farther than that around here and lived to tell it. Boys have a habit of living." While she talked she was gathering her things together. Before marriage Mrs. Doctor had received one year of medical training and in cases of sudden sickness or accident she always took charge until her husband could be reached. For babies no one would have anyone except Mrs. Doctor herself.

The Weares' house was on Palmer Avenue, the same street as the school. When they reached the schoolyard, Ralph was still lying on the ground but his eyes were open and his lower lip was caught between his teeth. Mrs. Doctor, nodding to Mr. Tyler and Miss Williams, knelt beside the boy and her square gentle hands felt along his collar bone, arms and legs as she asked questions.

"Hurt here? How about here? Here?"

When he gave a short swiftly stifled cry, she nodded and, rising, walked over to the principal who had stepped back a few paces.

"It's the left ankle—maybe sprained—maybe fractured. Who is he and where does he live?"

"He's Ralph Creighton, son of that engineer boarding at the Dickinson House. I sent one of the boys for his mother. She should be here soon," Mr. Tyler told her.

"I'll need something for splints." Mrs. Doctor raised her voice. "One of you children fetch me two long pieces of flat kindling wood."

Cassie left the circle of young people around Ralph and ran to the woodpile. Returning, she stood looking down at the boy's gray face and sweat-beaded forehead as Mrs. Doctor took a roll of bandage from her bag and wrapped the wood tight against the leg from knee to below the ankle. It must have hurt dreadfully—Cassie could almost feel it hurt—and yet he never let out a sound. When it was done, Mrs. Doctor patted his shoulder and stood up.

"Can't wait any longer for the mother; I'm going to take him home to our hospital room. It will be easier for Doctor to have him there."

No one thought of arguing, least of all Mr. Tyler, who had been one of Mrs. Doctor's first babies. And so Ralph was carried off on a schoolhouse shutter by two men who happened by and were commandeered. Then the bell was rung and classes were resumed.

When the older pupils were assembled in his room, Mr. Tyler faced them, eyes stern and mouth a thin line.

"Was this accident the result of a dare?" Dares were strictly forbidden on school premises.

No one answered. Except for Cassie, no one had actually heard Alfred's words but of course everyone knew it *had* been.

"I'll repeat my question." Mr. Tyler's hand tightened on the long ruler he kept on his desk. "Was this deplorable and perhaps very serious accident the result of a dare?"

Cassie squirmed in her seat. She wanted desperately to answer but to tattle on anyone was unthinkable. She knew even Mr. Tyler's son would never tell.

The principal changed his question. "Was anyone on the roof *before* Ralph?"

Again there was silence; then slowly Emma stood up. "I was, sir."

Shocked disbelief showed on the man's face and in his voice. "*You,* Emma?"

"Yes, sir. I walked it twice. Over and back." White and trembling, she sat down.

"Oh, Josie, what will he *do* to her?" Cassie whispered, clutching at her friend.

After a long chilling silence, Mr. Tyler spoke. "You will remain after school, Emma. I will see to your punishment then."

The rest of the school day was torture to Cassie and Josie as well as Emma. Their only consolation was noticing that not a single boy would sit with Alfred at lunch hour or speak to him. Whatever they felt about the dare, they obviously had nothing but scorn for a boy who would not own up when blame fell on another—and a girl at that.

When school let out, Cassie and Josie waited on the road for Emma. At last she emerged from the building, her face streaked with tears.

"What happened, Emma? Was it awful?" her two friends asked in the same breath.

"Yes, it was. He didn't smack me but he talked and talked. He said if Ralph had been killed it would have been my fault and that if he is lame forever, I'll be responsible. And in a way he's right—if I hadn't wanted to show off—it's almost like being a murderess!"

"It isn't and you know it." Cassie cut Emma's self-recrimination short. "It was the dare. He would have had to accept it anyway. Alfred shouldn't have let you take the blame. I'd like to skin him alive!"

"It would have served him right if you'd tattled," Josie said fiercely.

"I know," Emma agreed, "but I couldn't. Anyway, the punishment's not as bad as I expected. I just have to take Ralph's lessons to him every day after school until he comes back and help him to keep up with the class."

Josie's green eyes glinted wickedly. "Oh my! And Mr. Tyler calls *that* a punishment? I bet you suggested it yourself!"

"I did not!" Emma blushed crimson and turning her back walked away from them.

It was four weeks before Dr. Weare would let Ralph return to school but after a few days, with white plaster encasing his leg, he was allowed to rejoin his family at the Dickinson House. Emma took his school assignments there every afternoon and some of the other young people began to visit him, too, Cassie and Josie among them.

The first time Cassie went it was because Mrs. Doctor asked her to go, but after that it was because she wanted to. It was always fun and it wasn't just because of the big plates of doughnuts and the pitchers of cider either. Mrs. Dickinson, or "Aunt Hattie" as she was affectionately known, was a tiny little woman with a heart big enough to include the entire village. As cheerful as a chickadee, she made everyone around her feel friendly and at ease, and in her big front room jokes and laughter were as plentiful as doughnuts.

In the beginning Ralph always pretended to Cassie that his father really was a railroad engineer who drove a train. This joke broke the ice between them and they became good friends. Ollie Arnold and Joe Daniels had some other joke with Ralph. The girls never did find out what it was, but the boys laughed about it a lot.

There was music at Aunt Hattie's, too. Mrs. Creighton, a gay and charming woman with sparkling black eyes, was always willing to play the piano while the young people sang and she had a beautiful voice herself.

"She used to sing in concerts!" Emma found this out and passed the news along to Cassie and Josie one morning at school. "And you know what else? She has asked Papa if she can train a choir for our church! She especially wants us three to sing in it. And she wants everyone to dress alike in robes like the choir wore in the New York church she belonged to." Emma described the robes.

"What did your father say, Emma?" Josie was hopping with excitement.

"He said yes about the choir. But except for the Christmas services he didn't like the idea of robes. And he said they mustn't be required even then. Anyone who wants to wear one can, but the wearer will have to pay for it. Until the mortgage on the manse is paid off, Papa won't ask the church for one extra cent."

Cassie thought it would be lovely for everyone to dress alike in robes until she found out from Mrs. Creighton that same afternoon that the material for each would cost over three dollars. This was a shock and she couldn't hide it.

"It will be quite all right if you wear a white dress instead," Mrs. Creighton had been quick to assure her, but of course it wouldn't be all right. Emma and Josie were going to wear robes and Cassie knew she couldn't bear to stand between them looking different.

On the other hand, it wouldn't be fair to ask Pa for so much money when it was not actually necessary. Cassie sighed. Somehow she'd have to earn the money herself and she'd better find a way right now.

Leaving Mrs. Creighton, she started for Judge Donaldson's house on Main Street. The day before she'd noticed Jabez and Caleb and Noah, the three old men who lived in the loft of Aunt Hattie's barn, digging potatoes in the judge's flat, sandy field across the railroad tracks. Perhaps the judge would hire her to dig there, too.

Everyone called the three old men "the derelicts" because they had no families or regular jobs and just drifted around for the most part, picking up things in the woods or watching the trains go by. Jabez was the tall thin one with the beaky nose, and Caleb was red-faced and heavy. Noah had curly white hair and round eyes like a child's. Some folks said Noah was half-witted and made fun of him, but Cassie never did. The derelicts were gentle old souls and Cassie loved them all, especially Noah. If the judge would pay her to work along with them in the potato field, she'd enjoy doing it.

Then, standing in front of his house, she changed her mind. She remembered hearing the judge once say to Pa that he didn't hold with women doing men's work. She went on to the printing office instead. Sometimes Mr. Daniels needed help delivering papers or doing odd jobs. Anyway, if there was a job anywhere in the village, he'd know about it.

She found Mr. Daniels working at his desk, paper cuffs protecting his sleeves and a green eyeshade on his forehead. As she told him about the choir and why she

needed money, he peered at her kindly through steel-rimmed glasses.

"I do know of several jobs around town, Cassie," he said when she finished, "but it so happens I can use you myself. My printer has quit and I'll be glad of extra help while I'm short-handed. Come back tomorrow after school with Joe."

When Cassie reported for work the next afternoon, the paper was still on the press. The kerosene engine was running full tilt and the machinery was going slap-bang shhh.

"Paper's late today," Joe shouted as he led her downstairs to the basement from which the sounds came and where reverberations seemed to shake the walls.

Mr. Daniels looked up as he became aware of them but his hands still worked in rhythm, feeding one sheet of paper after another into the press. "Almost finished the outsides," he shouted. "Joe, show Cassie what to do."

Taking sheets, printed on one side, from the rack at the foot of the press where moving tapes deposited them, spreading them on long tables to dry, turning blank sides up and stacking them for the next run-through, Cassie followed Joe's instructions, given mostly in sign language because of the noise. Then, when paper printed on both sides began to pile up, she and Joe began to fold. About five o'clock the press stopped its bang-clatter and the belt slapped idly a few times as the engine gave its final whir. The *Katonah Times* for the week of October 5th, 1894, was printed.

Mr. Daniels wiped a smudgy hand across his forehead and gave the children a tired smile. "You did real well, Cassie," he told her. "I guess we can make out all right until I find regular help again."

Cassie was sorry for Mr. Daniels when his advertisements for a printer brought no results right away but she couldn't help appreciating her own luck. While he was short-handed she didn't have to worry that he'd let her go before she earned enough money for the robe.

Every afternoon now, as soon as school let out, she would hurry to the printing office where she did all sorts of odd jobs, like running to the door when the bell jangled to see who wanted Mr. Daniels, or running across to the depot for the outside news that came in over the telegraph wires. And, under Joe's supervision at first, she cleaned type and distributed it back into the partitioned drawers where each letter was kept separate.

Sometimes on Mondays or Tuesdays, which were slow days, Mr. Daniels even let her practice setting type. "Just take anything from the wastebasket and set the first lines," he'd say.

Once Cassie fished out a fashion hint: "*Jewelled gloves* are the newest addition to the toilet . . . it isn't good form to wear rings outside one's gloves," it read. Until she had it set, she didn't think about it, but then she began to laugh. She could just picture Aunt Hattie or Mrs. Doctor in jewelled gloves!

A day or so later, though, she found a crumpled clipping in the basket that wasn't funny at all. She didn't set it in type—she couldn't. Clipped from a paper in a nearby village, it was headed, KATONAH A PROSPECTIVE LAKE PORT. The words below weren't as sure sounding as the headline. Someone was only guessing that the buildings on the river might have to go to make room for a spreading lake, but this gave Cassie small comfort. Her heart plummeted right down into her stomach.

"Do you think it will happen, Mr. Daniels? *Do* you?" she asked, showing him the clipping.

Mr. Daniels told her that he had thrown the piece away as too irresponsible to reprint. "No one knows yet where the water line will be, Cassie. Not even Mr. Creighton. Not until the surveys are completed."

At the time she felt reassured but the next day when Mr. Daniels paid her the last of the money she needed for the robe, Cassie asked him to let her stay on.

"Why sure," he agreed, "I hoped you *would* stay on. Even when I get regular help, I could use you a couple of afternoons a week."

Cassie thanked him gratefully. In a future that could seem certain one minute and uncertain the next, she felt an unexplainable compulsion to store away quarters and fifty cent pieces in the candy box in her top bureau drawer, the way squirrels were storing nuts against the winter months. And there was more to it than that. News came first to the printing office. Staying on, she'd be likely to learn right away of any real threat to her happiness.

5

The Skating Party

Days as well as nights became chilly. Some mornings there were brittle fingers of ice reaching out into the river from the banks, and always, now, the iron pot-bellied stoves in the schoolhouse were kept burning. On their flat tops, pans of water sizzled and the smell of steam mingled with the smell of chalk dust and yellow soap.

Several evenings a week the choir met in the front room of the Dickinson House; when November turned into December they began practicing Christmas music. Aunt Hattie's boarders would gather around the coal grate in the back parlor to listen, and the three old derelicts would come in from the barn and listen, too, warming themselves at the big kitchen range.

Then, almost before Cassie knew it, the holidays were right around the corner. One Saturday night, in mid-December, Estelle Whitlock gave a skating party as she did every year when the mill pond froze solid. The entire seventh and eighth grades were invited. Strapping on her skates at the edge of the pond, Cassie glowered at Alfred. Most everyone else seemed to have forgotten the episode on the schoolhouse roof and how Alfred had let Emma take the blame. But she hadn't forgotten and neither had Josie and Emma.

"Cass-eee! Hurry up!" Josie, already on the ice, waved a mittened hand. Cassie's scowl vanished as she waved back.

The moon was almost full and the dark ice beneath it rumbled excitingly as it thickened in the near-zero cold. Dressed in warm woolens, with bright hoods or stocking caps on their heads and bright knitted mufflers flying out behind them, boys and girls were racing and playing tag and snap-the-whip. Buckling her last strap and drawing in a deep breath of icy air, Cassie skated off to join Josie.

"You're it!" Ollie shouted, touching her shoulder and speeding away.

"Cassie's it!" Estelle warned everyone. "Look out for Cassie!"

She set off after Estelle and had almost caught her when she fell. Estelle sped off laughing and Cassie, picking herself up, turned back to chase Joe Daniels. Joe was fast and she was just about breathless when Alfred cut in between them. He was temptingly close but she certainly wasn't going to tag Alfred; she didn't even want to touch him. Instead she swerved and tagged George Tyler. Alfred skated off alone, hands clasped behind his back.

Alfred was still skating alone when the young people playing tag shifted to snap-the-whip. Cassie joined Emma and Josie in a line led by two strong boys who could really make it snap hard. Cassie was next to the end, holding on for dear life, when Emma, at the very end, was snapped off and went spinning away. Still whirling and fighting for balance, Emma bumped into Alfred. Before she could fall he put an arm around her and for a moment they whirled together. Then with crossed hands they glided away from the laughing, shouting players.

Cassie could hardly believe her eyes. *Emma skating with Alfred!*

Another snap and Josie and Cassie both flew off. They didn't rejoin the game but stood watching Emma and Alfred.

"My - oh - my," Josie said slowly and as though she couldn't believe her eyes either. "Here we've been cold-shouldering Alfred for weeks because he let Emma take the blame for Ralph's accident and now she's skating with him!"

There was no denying that Alfred was the best boy skater in Katonah, just as Emma was the best girl skater. Like birds they skimmed over the ice to the far end of the

pond where black shadows hid them; then skimmed back into the moonlight and the flicker of the bonfire built on shore. They drew apart to make separate figures and came together again to waltz. Emma scarcely looked at Alfred but her expression was one of pure rapture as they spun faster and faster in swift, sure curves.

"How *could* you, Emma?" Cassie and Josie asked accusingly a little later when they were drinking hot cocoa brought down to the pond by Estelle's parents.

"I didn't really mean to," Emma replied, "but when he stopped me from falling and started skating away with me it seemed silly to make a fuss. Besides, he's the only boy who can do figures." Her cheeks were still flushed from the exercise and her blue eyes sparkled. Then, glancing at Ralph who sat skateless on a fallen tree by the fire, she went over to him with a worried little frown.

He tossed a pebble from one hand to the other as he looked up at her. "You're some skater, Emma. Alfred is too; I'll have to grant him that."

"I didn't really mean to skate with him." Emma started the same explanation she had given the girls but Ralph cut her short.

"It's your own business who you skate with, I guess."

"Ralph . . ."

With a flick of his wrist the pebble flew up into the air and came down on the back of his other hand.

Emma tossed her head and glided off to join Alfred again. His arm squeezed tight as he put it around her and she laughed up into his eyes self-consciously.

"Well, how do you like that?" Josie asked in disgust.

"I don't. Not one bit," Cassie answered. She couldn't have explained it but she felt as though Emma had suddenly grown years older and was leaving them.

The next minute she and Josie were pulled into another game of snap-the-whip. Emma and Alfred skated together the rest of the evening.

When the party ended, Emma took a long time removing her skates. First she fussed with one buckle and then another with unaccountably clumsy fingers while Cassie and Josie waited. At last, eyes still on the buckles, she said, "You might as well go on. Alfred won't mind seeing I get home safe."

"You wouldn't!" Josie exploded. "You just *couldn't* let him walk you home."

"It was bad enough to skate with him," Cassie backed Josie up. "If you let him walk you home, people will think you *like* him!"

Neither girl realized that their voices had risen so loud until Emma, crimsoning, implored them, "Hush—oh, please hush!"

Alfred was approaching. From his expression it was quite evident that he'd overheard the conversation, but ignoring the other two, he spoke only to Emma.

"Ready?"

"Almost." Emma looked up at him and then her glance went beyond to where Estelle's parents stood talking with a man who had just joined them at the fire. A worried look crossed her face.

The man had his back to them but Cassie knew it was Emma's father. The next instant she knew something else, too. Emma didn't want him to turn around while Alfred was looking at her the way he was.

The buckles that had given so much trouble suddenly became manageable and Emma, slipping off her skates, ran toward the fire. When she was close to it she called out, "Papa—oh, Papa, here I am!"

Alfred watched her leave with her father and then turned on Cassie and Josie, his face ugly with anger. "I heard what you said to Emma; don't think I didn't. You two stay out of my business, do you understand? If you don't you are going to be real sorry." With that bit of advice he turned on his heel and walked away.

"Did you hear that? Who does he think *he* is!" Josie exclaimed furiously.

Ollie and Joe came up, skates swinging over their shoulders. "What's going on?" they wanted to know.

Cassie told them what had happened. "We've got to do something about Alfred—we've just got to," she ended.

"Uh-huh." Ollie agreed. "But not on account of Emma. That's her affair. On account of something I just learned yesterday. You know how all the little boys have been tagging after Alfred lately? Well, I've found out why. It's a sort of Indian club and he's the chief. They have pow-wows, and you know what? He's teaching them to smoke."

"Corn silk?"

"Naw, real tobacco."

"Not Seth and Moses!" Josie cried indignantly.

"Sure, *all* the third grade boys—including your brothers."

Josie drew in her breath. While she was letting it out in a hiss, Joe spoke, "But why would Alfred want to bother with a kid club? And why teach them to smoke?" He shook his head. "It doesn't make sense. I don't believe it."

"Sure it makes sense," Ollie said. "Alfred can't buy cigarettes. None of the stores will sell them to anyone under sixteen. So big chief Alfred trades wampum with the kids for them. Nice round shiny wampum. Lenses for eyeglasses from his father's factory. The kids collect them. See?"

"But where do the little boys get cigarettes to trade?" Much as she disliked Alfred, Cassie was sure Ollie was wrong about this.

"Indian forays on the stores and markets."

"So that's it!" Josie exclaimed. "I bet you're right after all, Ollie. Pa has been missing cigarettes lately. Indian forays, my eye! It's just plain stealing. Alfred has been getting Seth and Moses to steal from their own pa."

Her voice rose shrilly. "Just wait until I get my hands on Alfred. I'll scratch his eyes out."

She looked ready to set off on that mission then and there but Ollie stopped her. "You can't, Josie." His round face was worried. "If you so much as say anything to Alfred, he'll know Jabez told on him."

"Jabez?" Cassie asked. "Is that how you found out?"

"That's right. Jabez was picking up sticks for kindling in the woods a few days ago. He was near a cave and saw smoke coming out. It was a pow-wow. He saw the whole thing."

"But did Alfred see *him?*"

Ollie nodded. "Sure he did. And he told Jabez if he even breathed a word about the pow-wow that he'd get all the derelicts put out of Aunt Hattie's barn. He could, too. Alfred's father holds the mortgage on the Dickinson place. Technically it's a fire hazard for them to sleep in the loft."

"How utterly hateful!" Cassie was appalled. Why, if Alfred had the derelicts put out of the barn, where could they live? No one but Aunt Hattie would be willing to take them, and besides they wouldn't be happy anywhere else. There must be some way, though. Some way to stop the smoking and stealing without getting the derelicts in trouble. Then she had an idea.

"If we should accidentally happen to stumble on a

pow-wow ourselves the way Jabez did, then Alfred couldn't blame him. If *we* see Alfred trading lenses for cigarettes, we can—"

"We can skin the little boys alive so they'll never steal again," Josie broke in.

"And we can keep Alfred worried for months and months for fear we'll tell Josie's father and the other storekeepers where their cigarettes have been going!" Ollie's voice was jubilant.

"And I can make him promise to stay away from Emma forever and ever." Cassie said this but it was to herself. The boys weren't interested in that part. They, and Josie too, were already on Alfred's trail in their imaginations.

"We'll have to take turns following him," Joe suggested. "We'll skulk behind trees and things, until he leads us to one of his pow-wows. Then we'll discover him in the act accidentally-on-purpose."

Josie was delighted. "We can have a secret club of our own. Spying on Alfred. Like—like vigilantes!"

And so the Katonah Vigilante Society was born. Ollie was elected president; Joe, vice-president; and Cassie and Josie, secretary and treasurer.

When Cassie reached home she stood for a while on the porch. She was still all riled up on account of Alfred.

Then gradually the turmoil quieted as she leaned against the porch railing, eyes on the sleeping village, love of it flowing through her.

Like glass the river shone voiceless and motionless in the moonlight. Not a branch moved on the saplings she had helped the Village Improvement Society set out in September. Not so much as a twig quivered. It was as though an ice witch had frozen a moment into forever. Nothing would ever change then, Cassie thought, wishing it were so. She and Josie and Emma would always stay the same age as they were right now. Emma wouldn't be growing away from them. The village wouldn't change either. Mr. Arnold would always be the postmaster and shoemaker, and not one house or store would be different. She stood absolutely still, not wanting to risk breaking the spell by moving even a finger.

Across the silver of moonlight a yellow light sprang out in a narrow path as Pa lit a lamp upstairs. Almost at the same instant the Arnolds' dog barked and from down the track came the whistle of a train. Unconsciously Cassie had been holding her breath. Now she let it out in a frosty puff of air.

"That you, Cassie?" Pa called down from his window.

"Yes, Pa." She went inside and hung her jacket and hood on the hall tree.

"Have a good time at the party, honey?"

"Sure, Pa." She walked upstairs and sat on the edge of his bed. "I was wishing just now that I could always stay twelve years old and nothing would ever change."

"Things have to change, honey."

"Oh, Pa, I don't want them to." They hadn't talked about the river for a long time—she'd hardly let herself think of it, but now she had to ask, "Pa, what will we do if the new survey makes the water level higher than the house and shop?"

"Shows, not makes, Cassie. The survey has nothing to do with raising the water level. It will only show what land will be flooded, if any."

"What if it *shows* this property will be flooded, then?" Cassie wouldn't be put off.

"Well, in that case the City would pay Mr. Meech enough to buy some other property in its place."

"But that wouldn't help us any, Pa. What could we do?"

He shook his head. "We can only hope that the level will stay the same, honey." It was the answer he had given before, way back in September.

"Pa . . ." Cassie hesitated and then plunged on, "Pa, couldn't we buy a little place somewhere in from the river? I have almost twenty dollars saved—I haven't told you, but I've been saving. Wouldn't that be nearly enough for a little piece? With what you have?"

Pa gave her shoulder a hug. "Thank you, honey, but it wouldn't be enough. Land's expensive. Meech offered me this at nine hundred dollars if I could have bought instead of renting, three years ago. Prices have gone up since then."

Cassie walked over to the window and looked down at the river. Ice and all, it seemed to be rising right in front of her eyes. "When will we know, Pa?"

"The first of the year, they say, but no sense in thinking any more about it till we hear. There's nothing else to rent in Katonah suitable for a blacksmith shop, but I have my eye on a rental in Pound Ridge. We can move there if we have to."

Cassie felt something simmering up inside her. If he had only put money in the bank instead of wasting it on his inventions and patents! Then maybe they could have bought a little piece of land. Suddenly tears came to her eyes and she began to shake all over.

"I won't *go* to Pound Ridge. You hear me, Pa? I won't go! I'll stay in Katonah even if I have to live in Aunt Hattie's barn with the derelicts."

"Why, Cassie!" Pa sounded surprised and real hurt but she didn't care. She slammed his door and ran into her own room, slamming that door also.

6

Tracks in the Snow

Of course in the morning Cassie was sorry, and she told Pa so, but the worry and misery remained. It was useless to try and put them aside any longer.

The first of the year, Pa had said when she'd asked when they'd know about the water level. On Monday she asked Mr. Daniels and he said the same.

"Around that time, Cassie. If the map showing the new level is sent me by the Commission before then, maybe I can print it in the paper the Friday before New Year's."

"Oh, please, Mr. Daniels, can I see it the minute it comes?" Cassie's voice felt tight as she made the request.

Mr. Daniels looked at her sympathetically. "Why, sure—no harm in that."

All the grownups had started talking about the water level again. Everyone agreed the land on which Meech's Optical Lens Factory stood would be submerged, and the buildings near the water at Whitlockville, but opinions differed on what else would go. Cassie heard snatches of conversation on the street and in the post office and even at the blacksmith shop, though Pa would try to stop it whenever she came in.

"Not likely the water will back up this far," he always said, but no one really knew except Mr. Creighton, and he wasn't allowed to give out information before the Commission was ready to make it public.

Pa always managed to sound confident, but he'd taken to hiring a horse from Mr. Meech and driving around the country when he wasn't busy at the shop. Cassie suspected he was looking for a place to rent and she started looking too—but in the village. She quickly found that Pa was right about there being nothing to rent in Katonah that he could use for a shop. There was only empty land like the big sandy lot across the tracks near the silk mill that Mr. Daniels rented cheap in the summer to folks who wanted to plant potatoes. So Cassie's search ended almost as soon as it was begun. That hope was gone.

School closed for the Christmas holidays. Cassie still worked at the printing office three afternoons a week, but vacation left a lot of extra daytime hours to fill. It seemed to Cassie during these days that she was living two lives at the same time. The first was the lonely one she lived by herself because all her friends were safe no matter what happened, and Pa kept pretending *they* would be safe, too, and no one but she seemed frightened. Then there was the second life to which she escaped—the exciting one where nothing was important except to catch Alfred red-handed. Cassie threw herself headlong and gratefully into the plans of the Vigilante Society.

Following Alfred hadn't led them to a pow-wow, so the Vigilantes alternated their tactics. Sometimes they stalked and sometimes they scouted around looking for clues. One morning, under a cliff west of the Rocking Stone, Cassie and Josie came on some cigarette butts in a shallow cave made by an overhanging ledge. They had come on it quite by accident because a light snow had fallen the night before and there were no tracks leading to it.

"Sweet Caps—fresh, too." Josie squatted down and picked up a butt. "Pa sells these. I bet this is the cave where Jabez saw the kids smoking with Alfred. Just you wait till I get my hands on Seth and Moses."

"No, Josie. You mustn't even let them know you suspect. If you do, we'll never catch them with Alfred."

Josie eyed the butt regretfully. "You're right. Besides we don't know for certain they were here. There's just one footprint that I can see and it's a big one."

Cassie crouched down beside her. Drifts had sifted inside the cave except at the very back by the rock wall,

where a print was etched in damp earth. As Josie said, it was big, and Cassie noticed that the boot that made it had been half-soled. Among the nails in the sole, one had been driven in a little crooked and out of line with the others.

For a while longer they scouted around hoping to come on large tracks accompanied by small ones, and then, giving up, they started gathering Christmas greens. When their arms were loaded with hemlock and red-berried branches of alder, they found themselves again near the Rocking Stone.

"Oh, do let's play on it," Josie suggested. "We haven't for simply ages."

So, laying down their greens, they scrambled onto its top. The thuds were slightly muffled because of the thin layer of snow on the bottom rock, but the booms were fine and satisfying. And moving from one end to another was slippery and hazardous, which made playing on the stone in wintertime even more fun than in the summer.

December 1894 became December 1694 and now the girls were Katonah's followers, Waccamane and Jovis, sending messages through the crisp winter air. Then Cassie slipped, starting a small avalanche that landed her on the ground. For a minute she lay there, not hurt but getting her breath, and looked up through white frosted branches at blue-blue sky.

"Oh, Josie," she sighed, in the present once more, "it's so beautiful. I wish it could last forever!"

"Well, it has, for hundreds and thousands of years," Josie replied literally.

"I don't mean the rock. I wish the *now* could last."

"Shhh," Josie warned suddenly, and both were very still. Quite near them a twig snapped, but even Josie on top of the rock couldn't see what had caused it. Then, farther away, there were more snaps.

Cassie got to her feet, trying not to make a sound.

"Of course it *could* be a deer," Josie whispered, but it wasn't a deer's sharp cloven prints that they found when they pressed forward. The prints they found had been made by boots, and large ones at that. There were no smaller ones with them, though, and the girls were about to turn away when Cassie took a closer look.

"Josie, see!" She pointed excitedly to the indentation made by the right boot. "It looks like the one in the cave!" She fished in her pocket for the notebook and pencil that all the Vigilantes carried, and sketched and measured the print. Back at the cave, they compared the sketch with the print left there. There was no doubt about it. They *were* alike, even to the crooked nail. If they hurried they would know to whom the boot belonged.

From the place where Cassie had made her sketch, they followed the prints, running until their breath came short and their ears rang. Then at the railroad they lost them. The rails, clean-swept by iron wheels, gave no hint of which way their quarry had turned.

"Shucks!" Josie cried in disappointment, "I bet it was Alfred, though."

Cassie looked to the north and then to the south. As far as she could see there wasn't a mark on the ties. "I do, too. No one but Alfred or Emma could walk the rails that far without slipping even once." Then she had an inspiration. "You know what else I bet? That until he saw us, Alfred thought we were some of the little boys on the rock—sending him a signal that they had more cigarettes to trade!" Her eyes shone. "The next time we hear it boom, all we have to do is sneak up to that cave and—"

"Catch him red-handed!" Josie finished the sentence for her. "Oh, Cassie, won't it be just perfect!" She gave a delighted hop. "Let's hurry quick and tell Joe and Ollie."

As they ran along the ties, they elaborated on their plan.

"Next time we see Alfred we will have to get him to walk in the mud or on snow so we'll be *sure* the prints are the same." This was Cassie's idea.

"Bet we could find plenty around Emma's house," Josie sniffed.

Suddenly, for Cassie, the Vigilante conspiracy wasn't so much fun. In forming a quadruple alliance against Alfred, they had shut Emma out, too, and she couldn't help feeling disloyal every time she thought about it. "It's for her own good," she'd always tell herself but she'd feel mean just the same.

As soon as they found Joe and Ollie, and told them their news, Cassie left the other Vigilantes and headed across lots to the manse. It seemed as if she just had to see Emma.

Since the skating party, Emma had been sick with a cold and hadn't been out of the house. She was still in bed, Mrs. Ferris told Cassie when she opened the door, but a hoarse voice from above belied her words.

Wrapped in a wooly blue bathrobe with a rag reeking of camphorated oil tied around her neck, Emma leaned far over the stair railing, yellow curls falling down around flushed cheeks.

"Oh, Cassie, I'm so glad you've come. Please, Mama, can't I get up? I haven't seen a soul but you and Papa and Dr. Weare since Saturday and I'm so lonesome I could just about scream."

"No, you can't get up, or even talk, if you want to sing in the choir at the Christmas Eve service," Mrs. Ferris said firmly, and then putting her arm around Cassie, "It was sweet of you to come, dear, but I can't let you stay. Dr. Weare says Emma mustn't try to use her voice."

Cassie smiled up at Emma. "See you at church then, and just wait till you lay your eyes on the white robes Aunt Hattie and Mrs. Creighton have made for all of us to wear!"

Walking down the steps she felt a lot better. All the time she'd been feeling mean and disloyal, Emma hadn't even known she'd been shut out. And Emma need never know. By means of the discovery she and Josie had just made, the Vigilante Society would surely catch Alfred before Christmas Eve. Then they could disband. One thing, Cassie promised herself. Never again would she join any alliance that did not include *both* Josie and Emma.

7

Signal on the Rocking Stone

It turned colder that night and the ground froze. Even the snow had a crust hard enough to stand on. Under these conditions finding a footprint that could be identified as Alfred's was not going to be easy, but none of the Vigilantes gave up.

Seeing him leave the barber shop the next afternoon, Cassie and Josie followed Alfred up River Street at what they'd thought a safe distance. Suddenly he turned and walked back to confront them.

"Quit following me," he growled. "And don't try and pretend you weren't. I seen you tagging after me ever since I left the barber shop. If you two know what's good for you, you'll skedaddle right now and I don't mean maybe!"

His face was red with annoyance and on the otherwise empty road he looked very tall. While Cassie was searching for a reply that would allay his suspicions, Josie spoke up pertly.

"Oh, pardon *us*. We didn't know you *owned* River Street. When did you buy it?"

Annoyance turned to fury and Alfred took a menacing step forward. Both girls held their ground, outwardly calm but wishing nonetheless that someone would just happen down the road from Whitlockville.

Cassie stepped off the road. "Guess we can get those alder berries here, Josie," she said, hoping her voice sounded casual and unconcerned. "Bye, Alfred. And don't flatter yourself that we were following you. Josie and I have better things to do than tag after boys."

She walked toward the river's edge and started breaking off twigs of alder. Josie came to join her.

"My, these are pretty, Cassie. They will look real nice in our wreaths."

Though they'd turned their backs they could still feel Alfred's eyes boring through them, as though he were trying to make up his mind. Then after a minute or two they heard him go on toward Whitlockville.

Both girls left off berry-picking to stare after him. Suddenly Cassie dug her fingers hard in Josie's arm.

"Do you see what I see?" she asked.

"I do. You needn't pinch me black and blue!" Josie

sounded aggrieved but like Cassie's, her eyes were bright with excitement.

Between the post office and River Street the ground had been packed and hard frozen, but a little way ahead was a boggy spot. Alfred had just walked through it.

"Oh, Josie, I hope—I just hope—cross your fingers, Josie!"

The girls waited another minute or two, to be extra safe, and then raced forward and flopped on their knees in the road.

The impression of Alfred's right boot was so clear, both in the mud and in Cassie's memory, that it was hardly necessary for her to compare it with the drawing in her notebook, but she did anyway. Yes, the ridge showing where the boot had been half-soled matched, and the crooked nail, too. There was no possible doubt. It was Alfred's boot that had made the print in the cave with the cigarette butts, and again yesterday near the Rocking Stone.

"Yipes, I feel like Sherlock Holmes and Doctor Watson both, don't you?" Josie squealed. "What do we do now?"

Cassie was just as elated as Josie that they had their proof, but she was worried too. If they'd really been Holmes and Watson, Alfred wouldn't have known they were trailing.

"We can't chance his catching us again or he'll know for sure we suspect. Joe or Ollie can take over, but I guess we'd better just lie low and wait for a signal on the Rocking Stone."

As they walked back toward the village, a covey of little boys, Seth and Moses among them, dashed past, skates jangling over their shoulders.

Josie's green eyes lit up. "Let's get *our* skates, Cassie! Vacation and ice won't last forever. Only a week more till Christmas, and then in another week school starts."

A week until Christmas and then a week until New Year's. Going on to her own house for skates after leaving Josie, Cassie counted the days again. Sometimes she felt she couldn't live till New Year's in uncertainty, and sometimes she felt the time wasn't long enough, because these might be the last days she could even hope that everything was going to be the same for her.

Then it was six days until Christmas; then five. Snow fell again. Cassie couldn't bear to be idle or alone. She coasted with Josie on the hill back of the judge's house; she went on rounds with Mrs. Doctor; and she helped Aunt Hattie Dickinson bake hundreds of Christmas cookies.

But whatever she was doing, every now and then she'd stop and listen for the boom–boom of the Rocking Stone. She began to feel superstitious about it; if the signal came before Christmas it would be an omen that the blacksmith's shop and their house wouldn't be submerged.

Three days before Christmas it snowed so hard in the morning that Cassie stayed inside. Then about noon it cleared, and after shoveling the walk she went up to Aunt Hattie's. That was the best place of all to listen for the Rocking Stone because it was the nearest.

"Mercy me, Cassie, you're as nervous as a witch," Aunt Hattie said around two o'clock. "You've dropped three sheets of cookies already and put lemon flavoring in the chocolate ones. Run along with Jabez and Caleb and Noah, and help them cut a Christmas tree. I want a real big one this year and mind you it's filled out all around."

So Cassie went off with the derelicts and they tramped through the snowy woods looking for the perfect tree. Among themselves the old men rambled on about the old days.

"Remember when the first train come through, Jabez?"

"You saw it?" Cassie exclaimed in disbelief.

"Sure did. It was in '47. Watched it from the Dowburg cut. Sparks flying out of the smokestack—them were wood-burning days. It sure was a fine sight."

"Oh, tell me more, *please!*" Cassie begged and so they searched their memories, as though they were attics from which they were bringing forth bits of the past to offer her. Most of their stories went back to the time before there *was* a Katonah.

"Everyone lived down around the mills in those days. Then, when the railroad come through, some thought it was smarter business to be next to it and they built new stores and houses around the depot. Except Ed Borley. He brung his old store with him."

"With him! How could he?"

Jabez cackled. "Well, we all thought he was crazy, but he did it. Rolled it on logs. Course his store was a small one and it got cracked up a bit, so it would have been almost as cheap to build new, but it got here. Still standing. Shed next to Putnam's store now."

Noah scratched his head and gave a toothless grin. "Hardly seemed we'd got settled when the talk about flooding began."

Thirty years, Cassie knew, but she didn't contradict. Noah often got things mixed up.

Then he fixed watery eyes on her. "I sure hope your house don't get drowned."

It was the first time anyone had spoken right out to Cassie about it and something inside her hard and tight began to melt. Tears started rolling down her cheeks.

"Shame on you, Noah. You've gone and made Cassie cry," Caleb chided.

Noah looked about to cry himself. "I didn't mean to say nothing I shouldn't."

Jabez patted her shoulder awkwardly. "Don't take on, Cassie. Noah had no cause to say that."

"I'm *glad* he did. Everyone else pretends nothing will happen to us, but it's bound to." She was sobbing openly now but she didn't care. Before these old men, pride needn't keep her from it. "When the land's condemned, we have no place to go. I don't *want* to leave Katonah. Oh, what can we *do!*"

All the old men shuffled their feet uncomfortably. Jabez looked at the others before answering. "We don't know, Cassie. Not any more than *we'd* know where to go if we had to leave the Dickinson place."

Noah plucked at his sleeve and whispered. Then, as Jabez nodded, he said, "Cassie, we'd be real happy to have you and your pa come live with us."

A week ago she'd threatened Pa she'd go live with the derelicts rather than leave Katonah, but even then, when she was mad at him, she'd known she couldn't do it. The lack of privacy in the hayloft would be hard on the old men, too; yet here they were, offering refuge with no thought of themselves. It made Cassie want to cry all over again.

Noah was looking at her in pleased expectancy, kicking at the snow like a bashful child, one boot gaping open at the toe. To hurt him was unthinkable. Cassie wiped her eyes and smiled.

"Pa and I would be . . ." she reached for the right word, "be *honored* to come and it's just lovely of you to be willing, but you see Pa needs a shop where he can shoe horses."

They all nodded understandingly and Cassie thought that Jabez and Caleb looked a bit relieved.

"Well, just remember you're always welcome."

"I will, oh, I will. You're the very kindest men in all Katonah."

It was nearly three o'clock when north of the Rocking Stone they found a tree they all agreed would suit Aunt Hattie. The blows of the axe rang out and then there was a sharp crack and a swoosh as the balsam fell through underbrush to the snow. The old men roped it and they were dragging it off when another sound came.

Boom—Boom—Boom

Cassie stopped walking and her heart echoed the booms until they ceased. Then she ran forward and caught up with the derelicts.

"Jabez! Caleb! Noah! Please help me quick! Find Josie and Ollie and Joe. Tell them to meet me back of that cave west of the Rocking Stone—Josie knows where it is. Tell them to come in from the north so no one will

see them. I'll hide on top of the cliff, in the thicket, till they come."

Cassie was almost out of breath. "Do you know the cave I mean?"

The old men nodded uneasily.

"If you can't find Josie, you'll have to guide the boys there yourselves. Oh, hurry, hurry!"

Leaving the Christmas tree, the derelicts started down

River Street toward the village and Cassie cut back into the woods and circled south and west until she reached the top of the cliff. She was so excited that she wasn't sure she would even be able to hear anyone approaching the cave, because of the thumping in her ears.

After what seemed a long time, though, she did hear something: a crackle in the underbrush near the cave below her. Cautiously she edged from behind a tree, trying to see what caused it without being seen herself. Suddenly, tail raised high, flashing its white flag, a doe bounded past her. Again the woods were silent.

By this time the derelicts must have reached the village, Cassie thought. Joe would be in the printing office, Ollie helping with the Christmas mail at the post office, and Josie might be anywhere. Would the old men find them? Then Cassie remembered something she'd been too agitated to think about at the time. The men had seemed uneasy at mention of the cave; perhaps if they couldn't find Josie, they might just drift off instead of bringing the boys.

Cassie's vigil seemed even lonelier now.

A rabbit hippety-hopped around the tree. Cassie was watching it embroider its three-point pattern on the snow when suddenly it froze. Steps were crunching in their direction. Cassie froze, too, and then with a surge of relief, realized they were coming from the north.

Joe and Ollie, shepherded by Jabez and Caleb, came in sight and she waved to them. Then a little later, Josie and Noah arrived. After an exchange of whispers they all settled down to wait in the thicket.

It was beginning to get dark and a cold wind had sprung up. Finally even Cassie had to agree it was silly to stay hidden any longer.

Joe approached the cave boldly. There was no one inside; nor had there been since the last snowfall.

"Are you *sure* you heard the Rocking Stone?" he asked when he returned.

"Of course I'm sure," Cassie snapped. She was tired and cold and dispirited.

Josie and Ollie said they hadn't heard it either, so Cassie made them come with her. When they reached the rock, sure enough there were footprints all around it and on its top.

"Yep," Josie said, examining them, "Alfred has been here all right. Maybe he *was* signaling for a pow-wow but maybe he didn't mean this afternoon. Let's watch the little kids like hawks tomorrow morning."

Saying good night, the derelicts started off for Aunt Hattie's in the gathering dusk and the Vigilantes returned to the Triangle, walking the rails and ties.

Pa was waiting in the kitchen when Cassie reached home. He had started frying pork chops and apple rings.

The smell was lovely and the room looked lovely, too. There were greens laced with red berries above the windows and doors, and a big wooden bowl filled with pine cones on the table. Over the back of a chair hung a string of popcorn and cranberries that Cassie was still working on to trim the little tree that stood waiting on the porch. Cassie breathed deep, loving it all, wanting to hug it to her. Then she saw Pa was looking funny.

"Cassie, honey, I have something to tell you." His voice was gruff and his eyes didn't want to look at her.

Cassie stiffened; every part of her rejecting his yet-unspoken words.

"No, Pa, no! Don't say it!" She didn't want to hear. She'd counted on Christmas at least before she'd have to know for sure.

"Meech told me. He bribed a man in the map office to tell him."

"Oh, Pa." Pretending was over. Her throat swelled and swelled but no tears came; nor any more words.

Pa's mouth opened but before he spoke the air was shattered by a strident call:

CLANG—CLANG—CLANG

It was the big iron hoop at the firehouse, sending out the message that never failed to bring fear to every heart in the little frame-built village. Only, tonight, Cassie's heart was dulled to all feeling but one.

Pa looked at her, misery in his eyes. "I hate to leave you, honey, but I guess the boys will need my help on 'Little Giant.' Wind like this, a fire's apt to spread every which way."

He pulled on his heavy coat and boots and went out into the night.

8

The Fire

After Pa left, Cassie didn't move until the smell of charred apple and pork was too strong to be ignored; then she carried the skillet outdoors and set it in the snow. Coming back she sank down in a chair by the kitchen table, resting her head on the red-checked cloth. For weeks, deep inside, Cassie had really known that the house and shop would be below the new water level, but the official decision was as much of a shock as if she had never anticipated it. She felt submerged, as though the river had already closed over the house and over her, too.

When the second alarm clanged around seven o'clock she only half heard it, and later she paid no attention to the sound of feet running up the path. The door flew open and a blast of icy wind swept through the room as Josie entered, too breathless to speak.

Cassie looked up at her with dull eyes. So Josie had heard the house and shop were going to be drowned. It was nice of Josie to have hurried right over but Cassie wished that she hadn't. She didn't want sympathy yet, not even from Josie. The tears that hadn't come when Pa told her the news were stinging against her eyelids now. One word of sympathy from Josie and she wouldn't be able to hold them back.

But Josie hadn't come to offer sympathy. "Cassie—a hose broke—your pa needs dry clothes." The words tumbled out in a rush when Josie finally caught her breath. "Hurry, I have to get right back."

Cassie went upstairs and set about finding the things Pa needed. Shirt. Coat. Socks. Gloves? Pa had no spare gloves without holes. She would have to send the green and red ones she'd knitted him for Christmas. She made a bundle of the clothing and, returning to the kitchen, put it into Josie's arms.

"Thank you for coming for Pa's things," she said. "He'll be grateful." It was hard to keep her voice steady and when she finished speaking she bit hard on her lower lip.

Josie looked at the bundle and then at Cassie. "But Cass, you have to come, too. Hurry and put on your coat. It's the schoolhouse. And they need everyone."

Everyone. Then it must be a big fire. Most times the men didn't want children around. Cassie sighed as she pulled on her jacket and hood. No matter how she felt she couldn't refuse to help. She took the bundle from Josie, followed her out the door and started running.

As they tore north up River Street, Josie panted, "School—it's done for—they're trying to save the Hoyt house now—if that catches, the Weares' and the manse will go, too."

School, Hoyt, Weare, Manse. The words echoed and re-echoed in Cassie's ears while she ran. Like the pounding of her blood, they became a rhythm for her running but they couldn't blot out the wordless misery in her heart.

Ahead the sky was red and as they neared Palmer Avenue the girls could hear crackling and small explosions like firecrackers. They tore on. Smoke swept toward them in a choking, blinding wall. On the other side of the wall a shout of alarm rang out. Cassie couldn't hear the words but the voice was Pa's. The next instant something fell with a crash.

Then every thought, every feeling but one was forgotten. Pa was over there, maybe hurt. Cassie stumbled forward. She had to get to Pa.

The wind shifted and the smoke wall retreated. When it was gone Cassie saw dark figures silhouetted against red; men on the hoses, men and women and children passing buckets from the river. She tried to pick out Pa from the others. She couldn't.

"Pa!" she screamed, "Pa, where are you?" Against the roar of the fire and the chug-chug of the engine, "Little Giant," her scream sounded to her more like a whisper, but Pa heard. He came. He wasn't buried under falling timber. He wasn't hurt. Just soaking wet, with icicles in his beard.

"Glad you're here, honey. We need all the help we . . ." Before he finished the sentence he had snatched the dry clothes from her and disappeared again.

"Get in the bucket line." Joe grabbed her by the shoulder and Cassie found herself between Seth and

Moses. The two little boys were sobbing, but working like grownups.

Reach—pass, reach—pass, reach—pass.

It went on and on. At first Cassie would look up whenever there was a crash or shout, but before long she could only keep going if she didn't try to straighten.

Reach—pass, reach—pass, reach—but it was Ralph now from whom she took the bucket and Ollie to whom she passed it. The little boys had fallen out without her really noticing when. Then, maybe hours later, it was over.

"They don't need any more water." The word from the fighting line was passed back from person to person the way buckets had been passed forward. Except for the school and a shed behind it everything had been saved.

Pa and some other men stayed on the rest of the night to make sure the fire didn't start up again, but everyone else went home. Cassie fell in bed without undressing. An instant later she was asleep.

In the morning she woke to the smell of coffee. Pa, his beard singed and his face red, but otherwise looking as though he'd spent a restful night at home, was frying sausage when she came downstairs. He started talking about the fire right away.

"It started in that empty shed in the woods back of the school," he told her, "but the shed was gone before anyone got there and the school had caught. We thought for a time we had that saved, but the wind was too much for us."

He piled sausage cakes on a platter and broke eggs into the sizzling skillet. "If the wind had settled steady, blowing southeast, it would have been a humdinger. Once the fire reached the Triangle, no one could have stopped it. Like in the fire of '74."

There was something that Cassie wanted to ask but Pa didn't give her a chance.

"Fire of '74 was started by a tramp. Constable thinks this one was, too. Soon as it was light—"

"Pa!" Cassie couldn't wait any longer. "Pa, when do we have to move?"

For a minute it seemed as though he hadn't heard. "Constable—he started looking around—he found—"

"Pa!"

Then he did stop talking about the fire. His voice had been excited like a boy's. Now it flattened. "Maybe a month, maybe longer. When the City buys the land from Meech, we may be able to rent from them for a while."

A month. Even that was longer than Cassie had expected.

"Does anyone except Mr. Meech know we've been condemned?"

"I'm not sure, Cassie. Why?"

"I don't want them to know. Not yet. Not till after Christmas. I don't want people looking sorry at us. Oh, Pa, I don't, I don't!"

Pa's hand went to the singed part of his beard, fingering it. "Likely no one will hear till the map is made public. Anyway, the fire is all anyone will be talking about for a day or two."

Pa was right. Cassie searched apprehensively for a sympathetic look in the eyes of everyone she met but no one seemed to have heard of their misfortune. Walling the knowledge tight inside herself, she went through Christmas able to act as usual outwardly.

At the Christmas Eve service, the choir wore their new robes. Emma looked like an angel in hers, and Josie like a minor cherub.

The church smelled of spruce and balsam the way it always did on Christmas Eve. The very little children, sitting together in the front pews, gazed up at the candlelit tree on the platform with wonder in their eyes, as they did every year while Mr. Ferris told them the story of the Nativity. Even the hymns were the same, though because of Mrs. Creighton's training, the voices rang out sweeter and truer, filling every heart to the bursting point.

Walking home with Pa afterward in the softly falling snow, Cassie thought maybe her heart *would* burst.

Neither of them spoke of this being the last Christmas in Katonah, but of course Cassie couldn't help thinking about it, and she knew Pa was, too.

They had baked beans and pie for supper, and then they lighted candles on their own small tree and opened their presents from one another. Cassie had washed and dried and rewrapped Pa's green and red knitted gloves and he pretended to be just as surprised as though he hadn't worn them the night of the fire. He had made her a ring out of silver wire and right in the center he had worked the letter C into a design. Cassie put it on and held her hand this way and that, admiring it.

"You like it, honey?" Pa asked. "I wish I could have afforded a stone, but—"

"I love it, I just love it!" Cassie interrupted, throwing her arms around his neck and hugging him tight.

On Christmas afternoon Cassie exchanged visits and gifts with her friends. First Josie came to Cassie's house and admired the little tree trimmed with popcorn and cranberries. Cassie gave her a pair of green wristlets bordered in red that she had made from the same wool as Pa's gloves, and Josie gave Cassie a pencil box. Then they both ran on to Emma's. Cassie had knitted wristlets for Emma, too.

The manse was filled with gifts, for everyone in the parish had remembered the minister and his family.

Home-cured hams, jellies and preserves, hand-embroidered carpet slippers and pin cushions, were just a few of the offerings. Emma herself had received mostly books of the edifying sort, but among them were others like *Little Women* that Cassie and Josie hoped to borrow.

After Josie left to deliver a present from her mother to Mrs. Doctor, Cassie proudly displayed the ring Pa had made her. It was then that Emma drew her upstairs and opened a bureau drawer.

"I've just got to show *someone,* Cassie, and I don't dare show Papa and Mama." Under the paper lining of the drawer was a little box. Emma opened it and slipped a gold ring with a tiny garnet onto her finger.

"From Alfred," she whispered, "isn't it just too romantic! Of course I won't dare wear it except on a ribbon tucked inside my dress, but I can look at it whenever I'm alone."

"Oh, Emma, you shouldn't have accepted it!" Cassie burst out.

"Why ever not?" Emma tossed her head and her cheeks grew pink.

"Because—because Alfred is so hateful, and besides you just said your parents wouldn't approve."

"Well then, I'm sorry I showed it to you."

"I am, too," Cassie said unhappily. "Emma, you can't really *like* Alfred!"

"Sometimes I do," Emma said. "And sometimes when he's mean, I don't. But he always makes me feel as though something real exciting is about to happen." Suddenly she smiled. "Let's forget this, Cassie. Anyhow, I could never like Alfred or any other boy the same way I like you and Josie."

The reassurance about Josie and herself brought a rush of warmth to Cassie's heart but she still felt troubled. She couldn't understand Emma's this-way-and-that feeling about Alfred. She only knew she didn't like it and it made her a little scared for Emma. She had a sudden urge to tell about Alfred and the cigarettes. If Emma knew he was encouraging the little boys to steal, she wouldn't even look at him any more.

"Promise not to tattle, Cassie." Emma was putting the ring away. "No one is really fair about Alfred. Papa and Mama think he is 'fast' but they can't give me any proof. Even I wasn't fair when he wouldn't own up about the dare. He explained it to me later. He was outside the window and if Mr. Tyler had started to strike me, he was going to own up."

Cassie turned away. It would do no good to tell Emma anything without proof. It would only make her champion Alfred all the more. The girls walked downstairs and at the door Emma said again, "Promise, Cassie."

"I promise."

From the manse Cassie went to the Daniels' to give Mrs. Daniels some Christmas cookies; then around five she went on to the Dickinson House. She had left it till last on purpose. Everyone always left Aunt Hattie's till last because it was the most fun, and this year it was especially important to Cassie to do the same things in the same way she had done them each Christmas since coming to Katonah.

As she ran up the walk she could hear singing and laughter, and through the long casement windows she could see the tree that she and the derelicts had cut in the woods. On the porch she stopped suddenly and stood still, looking and listening for a minute or more. She wanted to be sure she didn't ever forget a single thing about this last Christmas in Katonah.

On the branches of the tree hung the bright paper cornucopias she had helped Aunt Hattie fill with nuts and candies, and at its top, close to the ceiling, was the beautiful angel with spangled gauze wings. Beneath the boughs, on the floor, were piled toys and white-wrapped packages tied with red ribbon. Cassie knew one of the packages was for her.

She couldn't see the piano but someone was playing "Jingle Bells" and childish voices were singing the words.

In the center of the room on the big round table were tall china pitchers of hot chocolate and the cut glass bowl

Aunt Hattie brought out each year to hold the punch. Sandwiches and cookies were piled high on platters. A dozen or more of Aunt Hattie's friends and boarders were gathered around the table. Pa was there, talking to Mr. Fowler, and Cassie was glad she would be able to remember him in the picture.

The door onto the porch opened and light streamed out with a departing guest. Cassie went through into the house and was caught under the mistletoe by both Ralph and Ollie as she entered the big front room.

"We caught you fair and square, Cassie. Merry Christmas!" they shouted gleefully.

She blushed and scrubbed at her cheeks with the pretty handkerchief Emma had given her, but she felt such a warm rush of friendliness for everyone that she couldn't really get mad.

Jabez and Caleb and Noah came up to greet her and Cassie gave them the popcorn balls she had made for them, receiving in return a little doll made from a pine cone and hickory nuts. Later she found Aunt Hattie and gave her an orange stuck full of cloves, and tied around with a ribbon for hanging. Aunt Hattie hung it on the tree and said it smelled lovely. Then she gave Cassie a package that turned out to be a book, *The Vicar of Wakefield,* and sent her to help Ralph pass refreshments to guests in the back parlor.

There was some talk about the fire and guesses as to the amount of insurance that could be collected, but no one seemed even to know that the Water Commission had completed its map. Mostly the conversation was about Miss Williams who had just become engaged to Mr. Tyler's brother and was planning to be married in July.

Toward evening, Cassie found Mrs. Creighton alone and gave her the muslin bag she'd filled with rose leaves, cured last summer the way Mrs. Doctor had showed her.

"I'll make you another next Christmas, if you like," she offered when Mrs. Creighton sniffed it with evident pleasure. Then she caught her breath and bit her lip. Maybe there wouldn't even *be* roses at her next home.

Mrs. Creighton kissed her. "Thank you, dear Cassie," she said. Then she gave her an extra hug, holding her very tight for a moment as though wanting to comfort.

So Mrs. Creighton knew. Cassie left the party and walked slowly home. Christmas was over.

9

The Auction Sale

When she stopped at the post office on Monday morning, Mr. Arnold handed Cassie a letter from Aunt Sadie in Danbury, and gave her a message besides.

"Mr. Daniels was here a while ago," he told her. "Asked me to send you along if you came in."

She tucked the letter in her pocket and walked slowly toward the printing office. She hoped Mr. Daniels had an extra job for her but it turned out, as she'd more than half expected, that the map had come from the Aqueduct Commission. It was spread out on the big table by the press. Mr. Daniels, who was setting type at the shelf under the type cabinet, peered at her sympathetically over his glasses.

"Promised you a look, Cassie, but I'm real sorry you have to know what it says."

"I already know." She swallowed before speaking again because her throat was dry. "I want to see it, though. I want to see it on paper." Sometimes, in spite of knowing, she'd let herself hope there was a mistake.

She leaned over the table and ran a finger along the dotted line that showed the new water level. It ran behind Meech's Lens Factory where the Cross and Croton rivers met, and at Whitlockville behind the old mill and three houses. In Katonah, it ran along River Street, right through two sheds belonging to Poultney's plumbing shop and then a little farther south it swung east behind Pa's blacksmith shop and house.

No, there was no mistake.

"You've been a big help to me, Cassie. If I can help you or your pa any, all you have to do is ask."

Cassie straightened up. "Thanks, Mr. Daniels. If your lot across the tracks had a barn or something on it, I'd be asking you to rent it to Pa." She was surprised to hear her voice sound so steady and natural.

"Too bad it hasn't. I'd let him have it cheap. If you have to move, Cassie, come back and visit us often. Mrs. Daniels always has an extra bed made up."

Cassie was grateful that the first words of sympathy were those spoken by Mr. Daniels. She'd been afraid she'd cry when people told her they were sorry, but Mr. Daniels acted as though she were grown up and that made not crying possible. It made it possible the next day, too. By then everyone knew, because on Monday night there was a meeting at which Mr. Creighton told about the expected flooding all along the Croton and its tributaries.

Before Cassie finished washing up the breakfast dishes Tuesday morning, Emma and Josie were at the house. They flung their arms around her and Emma burst into tears.

"Oh, Cassie, it's just awful to think of this house being drowned. Whatever will you do?"

"Pa is looking for another shop. There's one for rent in Pound Ridge and one in North Salem, and Aunt Sadie wrote yesterday about a real good one in Danbury." Later Cassie repeated this sentence again and again but now it was new and stiff on her tongue.

"But you can't move out of Katonah, you just can't!" Josie protested. "It would mean we'd lose you. Like—like as if you died!"

"I can come back and visit," Cassie said, but in her heart she agreed with Josie. It would be as if a part of her, at least, had died.

"There must be *some* place to rent back of the water line. Maybe across the tracks," Emma insisted.

Cassie shook her head. "Not with a building on it."

Though the windows were winter-sealed, the clang of metal striking metal came right into the house. Pa was hitting something real hard on the anvil and Cassie envied him. She'd feel better if she could hit something hard and loud like that, too.

When the girls had gone, Cassie finished the dishes and tidied up the house. Then she wiped some finger marks off the white-painted doors, and toe marks off the stair risers. In all the time she'd lived in the house, she'd never loved it quite so much and given it so much care as during this last week and a half. Of course the furniture would go with them wherever they went, but even that wouldn't seem the same any place else. When she sat in the big wing chair that had belonged to Ma, she wouldn't be looking out at the Cross River or hearing the trains come through.

She had sat in it last night waiting for Pa to come home from the meeting, the way she'd sat in it waiting the time of the first meeting about the new dam. Only last night she hadn't cried. Perhaps she never would again.

When he'd got back around eleven, Pa told her what had been said. The owners of property to be submerged at Whitlockville were going to build new houses farther back on their own lands with the money awarded them by the City, and Mr. Poultney was going to put an addition on his store to take the place of the sheds he was losing.

The way Pa told it, it sounded as though everyone

expected to be paid more than it would cost to rebuild and nobody minded losing their old homes and buildings. Except Mr. Meech, and for the first time Cassie found herself on his side. Even if he were awarded enough to rebuild his Lens Factory on land farther back, its water power would have been lost.

He had spoken bitterly of crooked Tammany Hall politics and called the taking of Westchester water for New York City nothing short of robbery. He warned everyone that the assessors who would be sent up to decide how much the property was worth would be as crooked as their masters.

Three days later the assessors came. Cassie had been prepared to dislike them. She'd pictured them as sharp-nosed and mean-eyed, the way crooks should look, but they weren't like that at all. She didn't even recognize that they were assessors at first when Pa brought them into the house late in the afternoon and asked her to make a pot of tea. They looked just the way any other cold and tired men might look.

While they were warming up, they talked with Pa about the work they were doing. Though Pa seemed to know, Cassie learned for the first time that as soon as the assessing was completed and Mr. Meech was paid, the City, not Mr. Meech, would be Pa's landlord. By paying rent to the City they could stay on for a while if they wished. "Until the buildings are auctioned off," one of the assessors said.

At first Cassie didn't understand about the auctioning, but the man explained it. The houses weren't to be drowned after all, it seemed, and the City didn't want them either. The City only cared about having the land cleared before it was flooded.

"We let buildings go at considerably less than full value sometimes so we don't have to knock them down or burn them ourselves," the other assessor put in. "Some buyers sell the lumber and some use it, but whoever buys these buildings must have them off the property by the middle of June at the latest."

After they finished their tea, the assessors went about inspecting and measuring everything. Cassie couldn't dislike them, but when they wound the long tape measure back into its circular case, she felt as though it were days as well as inches that were disappearing. Even if Pa didn't find a shop somewhere else, they had only a limited number of days that they could remain in Katonah.

When all the property to be flooded had been assessed, dates for the auctions were set and Mr. Daniels was given the auction notices to print. These were for buildings up and down the Croton as well as on the Cross River, and though he had regular help now, Mr. Daniels asked both Joe and Cassie to work extra hours.

Cassie was glad to be needed for extra time. She had far too much of it. Until the school could be rebuilt, classes were to be held in an empty room at the silk mill across the railroad tracks, but there would be a delay in starting while the desks and chairs and other things lost in the fire were being replaced.

In the meantime Josie had seized on the prolonged vacation to visit her aunt in White Plains, and Mrs. Ferris had taken Emma to Atlantic City to clear up the cough that had hung on ever since the skating party. After Emma's departure, Alfred had attached himself to the fast crowd of young people who hung around Gertie Perkins up at Amawalk and seemed too busy for kids and pow-wows. Anyway, cigarettes had stopped disappearing from the stores and markets, and so for the time being the Vigilantes who remained in Katonah had disbanded. This left Cassie at loose ends, and work, even if it was connected with the auctions, was better than being alone.

One of Cassie's jobs was tying the notices into bundles for distribution, so she knew that eventually she would see the one for her own house. Even so, when it happened, it was a shock that made her fingers tremble and let the square sheets of paper slide onto the floor. It read:

AUCTION

FIVE ROOM HOUSE AND BLACKSMITH SHOP ON THE CROSS RIVER, KATONAH, NEW YORK, FORMERLY OWNED BY HENRY MEECH, TO BE AUCTIONED BY THE CITY OF NEW YORK, MONDAY, JAN. 24th, 10 A.M.

Abner Molton, Auctioneer

She read the words again and again as she restacked and tied the notices. The twenty-fourth of January, it said. School was to begin on the twenty-fourth.

On the day of the auction, Pa left for Brewster on an early train. He hadn't been able to work out a lease, either at Pound Ridge or North Salem, and the Danbury shop had been rented before he got there. Just last night he'd heard of something in Brewster and he didn't dare delay for fear the same thing would happen.

"I think you'll like Brewster, honey," he said, but Cassie knew she'd hate it, just as she'd hated the other places in turn when they had seemed likely new homes.

At the door he paused. "I'm glad you'll have school today, Cassie. It would make you feel real bad to stay around here."

The house seemed lonely after Pa left. When the school bell rang for the first time in over a month, it seemed even more lonely, but Cassie didn't join the other children; she had no intention of going to school. She went around touching walls and doors as though for the last time. She supposed that she and Pa would be given a few days to move out by whoever bought the buildings, but she felt this was really good-by.

Around 9:30, Abner Molton, the auctioneer from Croton Falls, drove up in a cutter, sleigh bells jingling. He tied his horse in the blacksmith shop and blanketed him before walking across the snow and up the porch steps.

"Whew, it certainly is cold," he said as Cassie let him in. "Don't suppose you'd have a cup of coffee handy?"

When Cassie brought him one he gulped it noisily. He was a big jolly-looking man and he gave her a friendly smile as he set the cup down.

"No sense in going outside till the crowd comes. You folks figuring on bidding the buildings in?"

Cassie shook her head.

"Well, that will make things livelier. If the former owner wants his buildings, no one likes to bid against him, most times. If he don't want them, I can generally get things humming. Lumber in these old houses and barns is worth something—especially to men in the carpenter trade. If folks start bidding against each other I might get them up to two hundred or so."

He took some papers out of a carpetbag and looked at the one on top. "Name's Meech? That right?"

"He owned the place. We just rent. Pa's the blacksmith."

People began to arrive. There were only twenty or so and Cassie recognized them all. Mr. Meech was not among them. The auctioneer carried a table onto the porch and laid his gavel on it. Cassie put on a coat and followed him out. She didn't want to join the men standing around in the snow, so she sat on the porch railing.

After joking a while, Mr. Molton banged his gavel on the table. "All right, folks, let's begin. It's cold enough to freeze the tail off a brass monkey and besides I have other valuable buildings to auction today. Now, who will start the bidding on this beautiful little house and fine blacksmith shop? Do I hear five hundred dollars?"

There was a burst of laughter and then Mr. Pettit, a carpenter, spoke up. "Quit your joshing, Abner. I'll give you five dollars."

"An insult!" the auctioneer howled in pretended rage.

Cassie felt herself growing angry. It *was* an insult. Five dollars! Mr. Pettit shouldn't even joke like that.

"Five twenty-five. The house will make me a good chicken coop." Mr. Hyke, a farmer, was deliberately baiting the auctioneer.

It was as though they were throwing mud at the home she loved, Cassie thought. She bit her lip hard.

"Five dollars and a half." Mr. Pettit raised the bid. "Ain't worth a cent more than that."

Suddenly and without realizing what she was going to do, Cassie raised her hand.

"Please, Mr. Molton, I bid twenty-six dollars." She glared down at Mr. Hyke and Mr. Pettit and all the rest. "I'd bid more if I had it," she burst out. "It's—it's *worth* five hundred!"

The laughter stopped and everyone looked at Cassie. There was whispering but no one made another bid.

"You hear what the young lady says?" the auctioneer shouted. "Worth five hundred dollars. Who will give me two hundred?"

He waited a minute. "One hundred? Seventy-five? Fifty?" Another wait and then Mr. Molton scratched his head good-humoredly. "So it's like that, is it? You had me fooled, girlie, but if your pa wants the buildings, I guess no one is going higher. Going—going—gone!" He banged with the gavel again. "Sold to the blacksmith for twenty-six dollars. Bring up the money, sister, and I'll make out the bill of sale."

"I'll get it; it's upstairs." Cassie almost choked as she took the stairs two at a time and her head was whirling. Would Pa be very mad? But she'd *had* to bid. And it was her own money. She counted out twenty-six dollars from the candy box, leaving only a few pennies in the bottom. The auctioneer counted the money again before putting it in the carpetbag.

"Bill of sale is all ready except for the purchaser's

name. What is your pa's name, Missy? What shall I write down on the paper?"

"Bates," Cassie said, her voice low, and then she repeated it louder. "Bates. Write it down C. Bates."

The crowd had already left for Meech's factory, the next place to be auctioned, and Mr. Molton untied his horse and got in his cutter to follow.

Cassie sat down on the porch steps and hugged her knees. She was still dazed by what had happened, but in spite of the cold she felt warm inside. She was a house-owner. She, Cassie Bates, owned the house and the blacksmith shop. The paper she held in her hand said so.

Until June no one, not even Pa, could move her from Katonah.

10

Cassie's Plan

Pa came home on the early afternoon train, looking well satisfied. He had signed a lease on the Brewster shop and a receipt for the first month's rent was in his pocket.

Cassie had been trying to decide how best to tell him about buying the house so he'd understand, but at first she didn't have a chance to get a word in edgewise. Pa was so full of enthusiasm that all she could do was listen while he talked about the shop in Brewster. She listened and even agreed that it sounded a bargain, but then he started talking about a flat over the bakery. It was vacant and just the right size for them to live in, he said. Cassie was sure to like it.

Cassie couldn't listen any more after that. She had to interrupt and tell Pa straight out about the auction and how she planned to stay in Katonah in her very own house until June.

For a long while afterward, it seemed as if they were

saying the same things over and over, though the words weren't always the same.

"But, Cassie honey, like I said, I've taken the shop in Brewster. Unless I move in as soon as the blacksmith who rents it now moves out, I won't get his customers."

"I know that, Pa. I know you have to go to Brewster right away but I won't be scared to live here alone. Honest, I won't."

"It wouldn't be fitting for you to live alone, honey." Pa was trying to be patient but his patience was wearing thin. Cassie could hear it in his voice and she knew her own voice was getting edgy, too."

"Only till school's over, Pa."

"Don't talk foolish, Cassie."

At last Pa sighed and got up from the chair tilted back from the kitchen table. "I told the baker that I'd bring you up to see the rooms this evening. If they suit, we will move on Saturday."

"I'll come and look, Pa." Cassie hated being on the outs with him. Besides, it wouldn't hurt to look and she hoped there would be something she could rightly object to about the rooms.

On the train riding up she sat with her fingers crossed, hoping so hard that she almost didn't hear when the conductor called out the name of their station. It had still been daylight when they left Katonah; now, half an hour later, it was dark. Street lamps were lit and, walking up the steep icy incline from the station, Cassie saw a street very much like Railroad Avenue except it was on a hilltop instead of flat ground. Pa pointed out the post office, hotel, and various stores and told her all the nice things he could think of about Brewster.

Children and grownups were hurrying past on the way to supper, just as they'd be doing at this time in Katonah. There were two girls about her own age, swinging their skates on straps and giggling about something that had happened at school.

Pa squeezed her arm. "They look a little like Emma and Josie, don't they, honey?"

Emma and Josie! Cassie glared at the girls.

The bakery shop was still open and the baker gave them the key to the rooms above and a kerosene lamp to carry with them. Pa unlocked the door at the top of the stairs and Cassie followed him into the front room. She hoped it would be too small or too something but it wasn't. It was large and square and, as Pa said, their furniture would fit it fine. They went into the bedrooms. Except that they looked out on an alley instead of on the river, Cassie could find nothing to complain about. One of the rooms had roses on the wallpaper, climbing up a green trellis, and Pa said that could be hers. He showed her how her bed would fit against the wall and her bureau between the two windows.

"It's real pretty," she had to admit, wishing all the while that it wasn't.

At the end of the long hall was the kitchen. The odor of fresh bread, drifting up from the bakery, gave the other rooms a pleasant sense of warmth but a stale sort of smell was coming from the kitchen. Approaching it, Cassie wrinkled her nose.

As they carried the lamp in and the darkness was flooded with light, dozens of loathsome black bugs scuttled for safety beneath the stove and sink and behind the baseboards.

"Pa! Did you see? What are they?" The horror Cassie felt was as crawly as the bugs themselves.

"Cockroaches," Pa said in disgust. "They weren't here this morning. They come out when it's dark."

Cassie shivered. "You mean if we lived here, they'd come out every night? Oh, Pa!"

He opened a cupboard drawer. There was a cockroach inside. He slammed the drawer shut. "Place is alive with them. Come up from the bakery, I guess. We'd have a hard time getting rid of them—maybe we never could." He sighed. "Come on, honey, I wouldn't ask you to live here. Tomorrow I'll look for some other rooms."

All the way back to Katonah, Pa didn't say anything more. His face had that miles-away look that it got when he was studying on a new invention. Cassie tried to talk but he didn't seem to hear, so she gave up and sat quiet, thinking. This time, on account of the bugs, she hadn't had to do any objecting to the rooms Pa had picked out but the next time it might be different. She had to settle things before then. Hands clasped tight in her lap, she planned what she'd say when Pa was ready to listen.

Pa, please don't look for any other rooms.

Pa, I simply have to stay in Katonah until school's over.

Pa, I just hate Brewster. I won't live there. I won't.

The little house on the river seemed prettier and homier than ever when they returned. After they'd taken off their outdoor clothes and hung them on the hall tree, Pa went into the kitchen and Cassie stood waiting, her heart pounding. When he came back she would have to say one of the things she'd thought of on the train. She'd have to stand her ground even if it meant hard words between them.

Pa brought two glasses of milk into the sitting room and handed her one. She got ready to speak but he spoke first.

"I been figuring, Cassie," he said. "Guess I can ride the train to Brewster till June. Maybe we can find a whole house by then. I'm real glad you bid in this place so we don't have to move right away."

She flung her arms around his neck and milk spilled on the floor. "Oh, Pa, I'm so happy!" She couldn't think of anything else to say, so she said it again and again.

When Pa went to bed, Cassie remained downstairs a while longer. It was twelve hours since the auction. For twelve hours the house had been hers—not Mr. Meech's or the City's, but hers—and during every minute of that time she'd been thinking how to make Pa let her live in it until June. Now that he'd agreed, she was exhausted as well as happy. She didn't want to think any more; she wanted only to be quiet and feel the walls of her house like loving arms around her.

Curled up in Ma's big wing chair, she felt her eyelids close. She jerked them open. Slowly they closed again. She slept until the moon, coming around to the west, lay across her face. Then she wakened, not all at once as she did in the morning but a little at a time as though a dream were still clinging to her. Only it wasn't a dream. It was something she'd half remembered just before opening her eyes.

Aunt Hattie had sent her out with the derelicts to look for a Christmas tree and . . . The memory began to slip away. Cassie shut her eyes and it came back.

They were walking in the woods. As though it were happening right now, she could feel the cold and hear the snow squeaking under her boots. Noah was right ahead of her, his white hair curling between cap and collar. Caleb was saying something about the first train, about the days before there *was* a train, or even a Katonah. Everyone had lived down around the mills then. There was something more, something important. She could see Caleb saying it but she couldn't hear the words. She herself asked a question but she couldn't hear those words either. Then suddenly and clear as anything Jabez replied. He said . . .

Cassie jumped out of the chair and stumbled upstairs. "Pa!" she called, "Oh, Pa!" Her throat felt all bubbly as though excitement was soda water racing through her.

"Pa!" She shook him but he kept on snoring. He looked tired, and older than he did when he was awake. Cassie went into her own room. She'd tell him in the morning.

In the morning he'd already left for Brewster before she woke again. After the first disappointment, she was glad. Maybe she ought to make sure she'd remembered right. Until then, it would be better not to tell Pa.

The school bell rang. Cassie had forgotten about school. It had no part in her plans for the morning, but when the bell rang she picked up her books. She didn't dare play hooky again.

It seemed as though everyone she passed on the street had heard about the auction and had a word to say. The grownups were mostly amused.

"Some little bidder, Cassie," Mr. Arnold said. "Your Pa was real foxy to leave it to you."

Emma and Josie were ecstatic. "Oh, it's just wonderful you don't have to leave right away!" Emma cried as she hugged her tight, and Josie spun round and round on her heel in joyous delirium.

Even Mr. Tyler seemed glad she was staying. "I am happy to excuse your absence yesterday since it will enable you to finish out the year with us," he said, smiling kindly.

Cassie was bursting to tell Emma and Josie the thing she'd remembered but she couldn't. Not before she'd made sure, and had told Pa first.

Classes in the silk mill were fun, with the big looms crash-banging overhead and Mr. Tyler and Miss Williams shouting to make themselves heard. Recess and lunch hour were fun, too. Here, on the flat lot adjoining the building, there was no "boys' side" and "girls' side" as there had been on Palmer Avenue, but the boys and girls had spent yesterday afternoon making opposing snow forts from behind which to snowball each other.

Emma was a deadly shot. Pink-cheeked and laughing, she let her missiles fly, making Ralph and Ollie her

targets as often as Alfred. To Josie this meant she was losing interest in Alfred, and Cassie hoped that Josie was right.

It was wonderful still to be at school in Katonah, sharing a desk with Josie again and smiling at Emma across the aisle, but Cassie could hardly wait for the afternoon to end. When the last class was over she grabbed her jacket and hood off the wall hook and raced out of the building before Emma and Josie could join her. Ten minutes later, after running all the way, she burst into the kitchen at the Dickinson House.

Jabez and Caleb and Noah were alone, gathered around the stove cracking black walnuts for cookies.

"Howdy, Cassie. Hattie's in the parlor thinking. She don't want nobody to talk to her," Noah said.

"It's you three I want to talk to," she told them and they all smiled at her in pleased surprise.

"Have an apple." Jabez offered her one from the big wooden bowl on the table. Cassie shook her head.

"Jabez—the day we cut the Christmas tree. You and Caleb were talking about a man who moved his shop from the mills to Katonah when the railroad came through. Do you remember?"

Jabez nodded. "Sure I do. That was Ed Borley. What do you want to know about Ed?"

"Not about him. About the moving and how he did it."

"On logs. What you figuring on, Cassie?"

She drew a deep breath. "I'm figuring on moving our house and the blacksmith shop back across the tracks where they'll be safe." At last the words she'd been bursting to say all day were said.

Caleb scratched his head. "Well now, that was just

a little building of Ed's that we were telling about. I wouldn't rightly know if you could move a house that way. I'd guess not."

"Oh." It was the only word Cassie could manage. She'd told herself not to count on moving the house till she was sure, but still she *had* been counting on it and her disappointment was too intense to hide. Noah looked at her in distress.

"Shame on you, Caleb. Now it's you who are making Cassie unhappy." The old man was remembering his own scolding when a month ago he'd spoken of her house being drowned. "I'll help you move it, Cassie. I'm real strong for a young man my age."

"I'll help, too. I'd be proud to try," Jabez said.

"If Cassie needs help count on me, too, but what's it all about?" Ralph, who had walked from school instead of running like Cassie, had just come into the kitchen.

"It's her house and the blacksmith shop, Ralphie," Jabez told him. "She wants to move them back across the tracks."

"Whew!" Ralph looked at Cassie. "You serious?"

"I was. Because of something Caleb and Jabez were talking about before Christmas. Only now Caleb doesn't think it would work with anything bigger than a shed. I guess—I guess I was just being silly." Cassie swallowed a big lump in her throat.

Jabez told Ralph about helping Ed Borley with his shop and how they had rolled it from Whitlockville on logs. Ralph listened and asked questions. Then he turned to Cassie, his eyes shining with enthusiasm.

"I bet it *could* be done, Cassie, only being bigger, a house would be harder to move in one piece. Let's ask Father."

He ran upstairs and a minute later Mr. Creighton joined the group in the kitchen.

"Of course it's possible to move a whole house, only it takes more engineering," he said. "Where are you folks planning to move it *to*?"

"Mr. Daniels' lot across the tracks. He told me once he'd rent it to Pa real cheap if it had buildings on it. Now we *have* buildings." Cassie was looking at him, tense with hope.

"Get me a pencil and some paper from my work-table, Ralph," Mr. Creighton said, and when they were brought he began drawing a rough diagram.

"Logs won't do. We will have to have heavy beams."

We, he'd said and *will*. Cassie's heart soared.

Mr. Creighton went on drawing. He put big cross-beams under the sills of the house, resting on beams running the other way, and stretching out in front like tracks.

Cassie leaned farther and farther over his shoulder

until her dark hair tickled his ear. He brushed it aside absent-mindedly and continued drawing. He attached ropes to the ends of the crossbeams and secured them to a single towline which led to an upright pole on a stand beyond the track beams.

"Your father could build the capstan," Mr. Creighton said, indicating this last object. "He told me once that he'd invented some new improvement for capstans."

The pencil moved on, hitching a horse that looked more like a cow to a bar at the top of the capstan. Then, with dotted lines he showed horse and bar moving in a circle and the towline winding around the bottom of the revolving capstan pole, drawing the house toward it over the tracks.

At last Mr. Creighton looked up with a deprecating smile. "I'm an aqueduct engineer, Cassie, not an animal artist or a house-mover, but I've seen houses moved in one piece and this is the general idea. If your father really wants to move the buildings, I'll try and help him work out the details. It will take lumber and men and horses, though. It will run into real money."

"We'll work for nothing." Jabez spoke for all the derelicts.

"So will I," Ralph offered.

"Pa can manage the lumber and horses. I know he

can!" Cassie had no idea what lumber would cost or horses either. And she didn't want to admit to Mr. Creighton that Pa knew nothing at all about the plan.

"Well, give him this sketch. I hope he *can* manage." Mr. Creighton rolled up the paper and handed it to Cassie.

"Thank you, oh, thank you!" Cassie gave him a quick, shy kiss. When Pa saw Mr. Creighton's clear and careful drawing and knew that he'd help, she was sure she could persuade him that moving the house and shop was a wonderful idea. In her mind she already saw them snuggly settled on Mr. Daniels' lot. She could live in Katonah, not just till June, but forever.

Before Pa got home she had just about time enough to see Mr. Daniels. She wanted to be able to tell Pa how many dollars a month "real cheap" actually meant. She was running out the front door when Aunt Hattie put a hand on her shoulder and drew her into the back parlor.

"Cassie, dear, do you recall what day it was that you helped select our Christmas tree?"

"The Wednesday or Thursday before." Impatient to be off, she wished Aunt Hattie hadn't stopped her.

"Yes, but *which* day?"

Cassie's mind was incapable of thinking of anything unconnected with house-moving. "I don't know."

"Try to remember, child. It may be important." Aunt Hattie sounded worried but Cassie, chafing at the delay, only shook her head.

"I can't remember, Aunt Hattie. Not now. Maybe I will later."

"If you do, let me know." Aunt Hattie sighed as she removed her restraining hand. A moment later Cassie was out of the house and racing toward the printing office.

11

Pa Has Visitors

Pa studied Mr. Creighton's drawing. "It's real interesting, honey. If we had money for lumber and rope and men and horses, I'd like to try it. But we haven't, so there's no sense thinking on it."

Slowly he rolled up the paper and gave it back to Cassie. "It was kind of Mr. Creighton to draw it out for us, and of Mr. Daniels to offer his lot for three dollars a month, but you shouldn't have bothered them, honey. You should have talked to me first."

An hour ago in Aunt Hattie's big warm kitchen smelling of apples, Cassie had been confident that moving the house and shop would be possible. Even half an hour ago when Mr. Daniels, too, had pointed out the need for lumber and horses, she'd been confident. Now, suddenly, her confidence was gone.

"If we could find a way to get the things we need

real cheap . . ." Her voice trailed off. It was hard to give up.

"If we *could*, honey, I might think different but we can't. The iron pieces, like bolts and spikes, I could make but the rest I'd have to pay dear for. You had best forget about it."

Turning away to hide her bitter disappointment, Cassie went upstairs and laid the drawing in her top bureau drawer beside her Vigilante notebook and the candy box —empty now except for thirty-two cents. If Pa said he couldn't afford it, there was no more to be said. And there was no sense in letting him know how bad she felt. Only last night, she reminded herself, she'd been almost beside herself with joy at the thought of living in her own house till June, and nothing real had changed since then. It was just something that she'd let herself hope for, and as Pa advised, she'd best forget about it.

In the days that followed, Cassie tried to put the moving idea out of mind but it was impossible to forget something that everyone else was talking about. She hadn't mentioned her idea except to the Creightons and the derelicts and Mr. Daniels, but word of it had spread through the village before she could stop it.

"I hear your Pa is aiming to move his buildings over onto Daniels' lot and give up the Brewster shop," Josie's father said as Cassie passed him on her way to school that next morning.

"It was my idea," Cassie confessed unhappily. "I hadn't asked Pa. He says we can't afford to."

"I'm sorry to learn that." Mr. Miller really did sound sorry. "People are going to miss you hereabouts. Besides, it will be right hard to do without a blacksmith in town. Old Bess lost a shoe yesterday and it took all afternoon to get her shod up at Golden's Bridge."

Over and over again, Cassie had to repeat, "Pa says we can't afford to," wishing more each time that she'd consulted him before speaking to anyone else. Even when everyone knew they were not going to move the buildings, talk of it still continued.

Now that Pa was working in Brewster, it seemed as though all at once every horse in Katonah needed shoeing and every wagon needed repairing. After church on Sunday, she and Pa were surrounded by people, all wanting to tell him how much they wished he could see his way clear to move the buildings and set up shop in Katonah again.

"Makes a man feel proud to know he's missed," Pa said later as he and Cassie were walking home across the snow-covered bridge. "If there only *was* some way to afford—watch out, Cassie!" Jingling bells warned them of an approaching sleigh and they drew over to the side of the bridge to let it pass.

When it had gone by, Pa began right away to talk about the sermon, but Cassie only half listened. *If there only was a way.* But of course there wasn't, any more than there was a way to stop the talk that made it increasingly hard for her to accept the fact that she'd have to leave Katonah in June.

Acceptance wasn't made any easier by Josie. Nearly every day she came to school with a new and impractical scheme that would allow Cassie to remain. The morning that Mr. Tyler showed them plans for the new two-storied schoolhouse to be built on the former site, Josie could hardly wait for recess to burst out:

"Cassie, you just can't leave. You simply *have* to go to the new school next year. During arithmetic class I thought of a way. Just listen. Dead trees don't cost money. If we let the little boys join the Vigilantes they can help us find real big trees that have fallen down in the woods."

All morning Cassie had been listening to Mr. Tyler describe the new school. All morning she had been feeling more and more left out. She felt bad enough already and silly suggestions weren't going to help any.

"Please, *please* forget about the moving!" she snapped. Then because she'd begun to let out her pent-up feelings, she went on to demolish Josie's scheme piece by piece.

"Everyone knows dead trees are no good for a job like this. And how could anyone be stupid enough to suggest letting the little boys join the Vigilantes, when it's to stop their stealing cigarettes for Alfred that we started it!"

Josie looked hurt and then angry. "Well, if you're so smart, I should think you'd know all that has stopped. The kids won't have anything more to do with Alfred. None of them." She turned on her heel and stalked off.

Cassie ran after her. "Josie, I was a pig. Forgive me."

Josie didn't reply and stared straight ahead.

"Josie, please forgive me. There's no reason you should have known about dead trees."

The bell announcing the end of recess began to ring and the snowball battle going on across the yard between the boys' fort and the girls' fort stopped.

"Josie, I'm glad Moses and Seth have quit stealing," Cassie pleaded.

Josie slowed her steps and turned. "Oh, Cassie, I'm a pig too!" Her green eyes were filled with tears, and Cassie's cheeks were damp as, arms around each other, the two girls went back into the building.

"Don't let's ever fight again," Cassie whispered behind the raised lid of their desk.

"Never," Josie agreed.

It was no wonder, Cassie thought, that she hadn't noticed the little boys had quit Alfred. She'd been thinking so much about Pa. After the first week of riding the train, he should have become used to it, Cassie figured. But he didn't act used to it. He'd scarcely speak at supper and he looked so dragged out that Cassie couldn't bear to pester him about things like fixing the broken latch on the cellar door or remembering to put housekeeping money in the blue sugar bowl. She fixed the latch as best she could herself and when she bought things at stores, she said she'd bring the money next time.

Pa didn't complain about being tired; Cassie knew he never would. He'd promised they could live in Katonah till June and it wasn't Pa's way to complain about something he'd promised. That didn't make Cassie feel any better, though. She knew she should offer to try living in Brewster, tell Pa to look some more for a place near his shop, but she couldn't bring herself to make the offer. She wanted too much to stay on right in her own house as long as she could.

Then one evening when she was doing her lessons, Pa interrupted to ask if she still had the drawing that Mr. Creighton had made.

"Why, sure, Pa, it's in my bureau," she told him.

As she ran upstairs, she wondered if Mr. Creighton

had asked to have it returned, but it wasn't that. When she brought it to Pa, he spread it out on the table and bent over it. Minute after minute passed. Finally he raised his head.

"Honey, I'm going to try it."

At first Cassie couldn't believe she'd heard right. Move the buildings? When he'd said from the first it would cost too much? When for days and days, a while back, she'd had to tell everyone they couldn't afford it?

"Yep, I'm going to turn house-mover." He slapped his knee a resounding whack. Cassie stared at him, not knowing what to say. Was he so plumb worn out that he'd forgotten about cost? Was he lightheaded? And if he was, who was to blame? She, Cassie Bates. Suddenly, the offer she hadn't been able to make burst out.

"Pa, I'll move to Brewster. I know that riding the train is too much, I've known it quite a while but I pretended not to. You won't have to do it any more, Pa; I'll come and live in Brewster."

Pa looked touched but also surprised. "Why, thanks, honey, but trains haven't anything to do with it. It's business. I've hardly had a customer in the Brewster shop."

Then Cassie began to understand. "Maybe there hasn't been time, Pa," she tried to encourage him.

"Nope. Ain't that. The blacksmith I took over from

drank. All his customers left him when a new man moved in up the road. Everyone likes the new man and there's not enough work for us both. I was bamboozled."

His voice, which had become bitter at the last, changed. "Now here in Katonah I have a fine business still waiting, but it won't wait forever. Some man with money to buy is bound to move in. I'd best set up shop here again before it's too late."

Cassie opened her mouth to speak but Pa didn't give her a chance. He went right on talking and his eyes began to shine with enthusiasm.

"I have a jack already invented that should do even the heavy lifting, and that improvement for capstans I told you about a while back should make it easier on the horses. Seems as though a lot of inventions I haven't been able to sell will come in real useful for the moving."

"But money, Pa?" Cassie was finally able to get the question in. "Where are we going to get the money?" Didn't Pa know the sugar bowl had been empty for weeks?

"Meech." Pa grimaced as he said the name. "Should have thought of him before. The old skinflint charges 20 per cent on mortgages but I guess we can meet the interest if we cut down on other things."

Cassie felt all churned up inside. She wanted to share

Pa's optimism but she didn't dare. Not yet; not till they really had the money.

Pa was studying her face. "What's the matter, honey?" His voice had become uncertain and a little hurt. "Don't you want me to try moving the buildings? Are you scared all at once that I'm not smart enough?"

"Oh no, Pa! Oh no! Of course I'm not scared. It's just that I can't seem to believe . . ." Then she was in his lap and he was hugging her tight.

"Will Mr. Meech really give us a mortgage, Pa?" Cassie lifted her head from his shoulder.

"Sure thing, honey. I'll go see him right now. No time like the present." Pa loosened his arms from around her.

"Don't wait up, honey," he said, shrugging into his heavy coat. "I might be late."

Nothing on earth would have persuaded Cassie to go to bed before her father's return. She tried to finish her schoolwork but she couldn't, so she gave it up and went to sit in Ma's big wing chair. Cassie didn't really remember her mother, but sometimes when she sat in the chair it seemed as though the mother Pa told about was close. Right now she needed her.

The clock had just finished striking ten when she heard Pa's steps on the porch. Even before she saw his face, she knew what had happened.

"He wouldn't give me the money, Cassie. Said he was right sorry not to oblige a neighbor. Said it wasn't good business to take a mortgage on buildings set on rented land."

Pa looked so downcast that Cassie knew he'd never doubted that Meech would let him have the money. It wasn't fair of Mr. Meech to have done this to Pa! She jumped to her feet, sending the chair sliding backward on the waxed floor.

"That's no cause to refuse. He's just being mean to make us feel small!" Her dark eyes snapped and hot color rushed to her cheeks. "We always paid rent on time, even when it was hard. He knows you'd pay up."

Pa just allowed that Mr. Meech was probably right but he didn't want to talk any more about it. He went off to bed and the next morning he took the train as usual to Brewster. Every morning he did the same and no one but Cassie knew that he sat all day in an empty shop. After supper each night he'd drag himself upstairs to bed more exhausted than if he had shod twenty horses.

Now that she knew Pa wasn't making any money, Cassie worried about it all the time. When she'd thought Pa had just forgotten to bring money home she hadn't minded so much, promising to pay later, when she shopped. Now it made her feel uncomfortable and a little sick, as though she were cheating. Part of the wages Mr. Daniels paid her she used for food, but she couldn't use it all because she had to save part for land rent to the City.

She stopped going into stores where she'd owed for several weeks, and she began crossing to the other side of the street rather than pass anyone to whom they were in debt. She didn't know what she could say if she were asked to settle up. She hoped—almost desperately she hoped—that no one would come right out and speak to Pa about paying until he got some work.

When a knock came on the door one very cold evening and she opened it up, her heart flopped over and started sinking right down through her stomach. There was no sense hoping any more. The moment she'd been dreading was here. Outside were Mr. Miller (it was seven dollars and six cents they owed at his market); Mr. Arnold (she'd promised days ago to bring him fifty cents for resoling Pa's shoes); Mr. Armstrong (three dollars for milk); and Mr. Hoyt (Pa owed him for horseshoe nails). It was the sight of the judge, however, that scared her most. The judge hadn't fully resumed law practice after retiring from the bench but occasionally he took a case for a friend. If they'd brought the judge along, it must mean they were going to sue Pa.

She stared at them, unable to find her voice. How

could they do such a thing? Mr. Meech might, if they'd owed him money, but these were all Pa's friends. And it wasn't as though he'd set out to cheat them—he'd pay just as soon as he could.

"Cassie, will you tell your father that we'd like to see him, please?" The judge didn't sound angry, but then he never did. Folks said even when he gave a death sentence once, he'd spoken just as usual.

Wildly Cassie cast around in her mind for some way to refuse. Pa had gone upstairs. Could she say he was out? Or that he was sick?

From above, Pa called down. "Cassie, honey, ask the

gentlemen in before they freeze. I'll be with them in a minute."

She showed them into the front room and carried her schoolbooks into the kitchen, spreading her geography out open on the table.

Idaho is bounded on the north by British Columbia; on the west by Washington and Oregon.

Suppose they put Pa in jail? There wasn't a real jail in Katonah—just the lockup in the constable's cellar—so they'd probably take him to White Plains. Where would she get the money to visit him?

On the east by Montana and Wyoming. On the south by Nevada and Utah.

How could they do such a thing to Pa? Why, Mr. Miller was her best friend's own father. Well, she'd never speak to Josie again. That was certain.

Its resources are gold, silver, lead . . .

The front door opened and closed again. She heard the stamp of feet as some more men shook snow from their boots before entering, but she couldn't see who they were. Pa must owe even more money than she'd thought. Cassie closed her book and shoved it away.

For a while all that the men talked about was the weather and the new school, and Pa seemed real happy to have company. He didn't know yet why they'd come. It was awful. Like a whole room full of cats playing with one mouse. Why didn't they stop it and *tell* him?

Then there was silence and the judge cleared his throat. Cassie's hands gripped the edge of the kitchen table. She wished she could be with Pa when they told him but she knew it would shame him to have her there.

"Mr. Bates," the judge said, "we are here because we can't do without a blacksmith in Katonah any longer. We want you to come back and set up shop again. All the people who own horses feel the same. If you will come back from Brewster, we will help you move your buildings back from the river."

Cassie didn't hear what Pa said because all at once there was such a buzzing in her head that she couldn't hear anything. She gripped the table edge harder—harder—so it wouldn't float away.

After a little, words and then sentences were clear again. Mr. Miller said Pa could have the loan of Old Bess for the capstan and that every horse in Katonah except those in Meech's livery stable had been offered for turns on it.

Mr. Creighton said the City intended to cut down the trees between their house and the river in June anyway, and they'd agree to let Pa buy them cheap if he wanted to do the cutting any time between now and then.

Mr. Haley, who owned the sawmill at Whitlockville, offered to saw them up into the sizes Pa wanted, and

Mr. Hoyt offered as much rope as was needed from his store.

Mr. Arnold spoke last. He said he'd figured that shoes and postage stamps wouldn't help much in the moving so he'd taken a paper around and got the names of all those men who agreed to work for nothing if it would bring Pa back to set up shop.

In a lovely daze Cassie listened to all the plans. But it wasn't the details she was interested in. It was the glorious fact that they were going to stay in Katonah.

She could hardly wait for the men to leave so she and Pa could share their happiness together. Finally the door shut on the last of them and Pa came out into the kitchen, his step light and quick, and his eyes shining.

"You heard what they said, honey?" He lifted her off her feet and whirled her around in the air.

"Oh yes, Pa, I heard. I heard all right! I guess we have the very best friends in the whole wide world."

12

House-on-the-Move

"Oh, Cassie, I'm so excited I can hardly breathe!" Josie's mittened fingers dug hard into Cassie's right arm. "Even Old Bess is excited."

This last remark was an exaggeration. Standing patiently hitched to the capstan bar, the Millers' big brown mare looked as calm as though it were the accustomed grocery wagon she was about to draw.

It had taken a full week of preparation to ready the house for moving but at last it was done, and most of Katonah was gathered to watch it take its first step toward its new location. Jacked up above its old foundation, crossbeams bolted to the carrying beams running under them, six heavy timbers laid out in front like tracks, it waited now only for Pa to give the word.

Emma, standing on Cassie's other side, stamped her feet to warm them.

"I do wish they'd start moving instead of just walking around."

Cassie wished so, too. It seemed to take hours for Pa and Mr. Creighton to make their last inspection. They walked the length of the timber tracks, prodding the railroad ties that served as cribbing beneath the tracks, holding them level. Then, satisfied that they were firm, the two men went on to inspect the iron spikes driven down into the frozen ground to keep the capstan from tipping.

"Gee whillikens, I'm glad it's Saturday!" Seth cried, running up to his sister Josie. "I was scared all week they'd be ready to start while we were in school."

Jabez and Caleb joined the young people and Jabez gave Cassie a fragrant, napkin-covered basket. "Doughnuts," he told her. "Hattie thought you might get hungry."

He moved away among the crowd but Caleb remained. "Noah wanted to come, too, only he was scairt," he said.

Now Mr. Creighton and Pa were walking back toward the house. Ralph walked behind them with a large cake of yellow laundry soap in his hand. Every once in a while his father would point down and Ralph would stoop to rub a place that had been missed when the timbers had been soaped earlier. Cassie followed them with her eyes and most of her mind.

"Why should anyone be scared?" Josie asked Caleb. "With Bess doing the pulling and Mr. Bates and Mr. Creighton the bossing, everything has *got* to be all right."

" 'Tain't that, Josie. Constable's been bothering Noah to remember something he's forgot. He's feared if he sees him here, he'll start asking again. It hurts Noah's head when he can't remember."

Pa reached under the house and felt each rope where it was knotted. All morning long everyone had been waiting for him to give the word to start, but even so it seemed sudden and unexpected when he stood up and called out.

"All right, Miller. You can start Bess around."

Josie broke from the crowd and hurled herself at her father. "Please, please let me drive her!" Then she added generously, "Cassie too—it's her house."

Mr. Miller looked at Pa and Pa nodded. "If they lead her instead, it should be all right."

"Start her slow and easy, girls," Mr. Miller admonished, tying the long reins up out of the way, but it was unnecessary advice. Bess always worked slow and easy. She was the most sensible horse in all Katonah.

One on either side of her head, the girls urged her forward. Bess settled into her collar, and her traces tightened as she started on the first of many circles around the capstan. The first time the girls led Bess over the rope on the ground it was slack, but the second time around it was taut. Bess was straining forward against her collar now, but still working steadily.

"House is moving!" A cry went up from the crowd, but Cassie couldn't see it move until Bess had made another half-circle and they faced it.

Slowly, very slowly, the building was sliding forward on its foundation.

"Whoa up!" The girls tightened their hold on the bridle but Bess had stopped the moment the command was given.

Mr. Creighton and Pa disappeared under the house.

Had anything gone wrong? Cassie's heart skipped a beat. She couldn't bear for Pa to have something go wrong right at the start. But no, the two men reappeared looking satisfied and called out to start up again.

Once more the circling began. Each time around, when Cassie faced the house, she could see it was farther forward, though still partly over the foundation. Each time around, the rope between house and capstan shortened. Cassie didn't count the number of circles they walked, she and Josie with Bess between them. As her feet tramped a harder and harder path in the snow, her thoughts darted from the plodding horse to the kitchen of the house. Had she made the blue sugar bowl safe so it wouldn't fall and break if the house tipped? Was the fire in the range really out or would a spark jump out if the coal door flew open?

"She's all of her on the tracks now." Mr. Miller put a hand on Cassie's shoulder as the crowd let out a cheer. "Your Pa has done it! She didn't tip even a mite."

Pride in Pa almost choked Cassie. Of course she'd had faith in him right along but that hadn't prevented some anxious moments. Now, until the second and third pair of timbers were traversed and the first and second brought forward and leveled to make new track, there was nothing more to worry about.

Some of the people went home or to work but some, including all the young people, stayed. With her mind free of worry, Cassie began to hear snatches of conversation as she continued to circle the capstan. She would pick up part of a sentence and lose the rest as she came abreast of a different conversation farther around the circle.

". . . Mr. Bates says it will take a week or more and then they will move the shop."

"I hear they are going to go right on *living* in the house. Imagine how . . ."

"No, I can't. Papa won't let me. He says . . ." It was Emma's voice now and turning her head, Cassie saw it was Alfred to whom she was talking.

"Good to have a blacksmith around. My horse . . ." Cassie was listening to the first conversation again.

"I always use nine eggs. It makes all the difference."

Then Alfred's voice. "Aw, Emma, it would be fun and who'd ever know?"

Every time they approached Alfred, Cassie found herself wanting to hurry Bess, but Josie, on the inside of the circle and apparently hearing nothing, held the old mare at a steady pace.

"I hear that fellow from the Department of Public Works was noseying around yesterday up where Birch Stream runs into the river. Other . . ." The rest of Mr. Fowler's words were lost in the continuation of the recipe. Before Cassie had time to learn exactly how much grated orange rind was needed, they had gone forward another quarter circle.

"Oh, Alfred, you know I want to, only Papa . . ." Emma's voice was so low that Cassie could hardly hear it, but Alfred's laugh stayed in her ears even when she and Bess and Josie had come up with Mr. Fowler again.

"Whoa, now," Pa called. Bess halted and Mr. Miller unhitched her traces and threw a blanket over her back.

"Want to use her again?" he asked.

Pa glanced up at the sun. It was directly overhead. "No. No thank you, Will. The judge has promised his Prince for this afternoon."

The house was almost at the end of the last set of timbers. It looked strange and somehow lonely sitting so high way up there, Cassie thought.

"Pa, can I go in? Will it be all right?"

"Why, sure, Cassie. It's as steady as a rock. And fix us something to eat, honey. I'm hungry as a bear."

Cassie patted Bess and swung herself up on the porch. Her hand was on the doorknob when she remembered. "Aunt Hattie made us some doughnuts. You can start on them. They're in a basket. I left it with Emma."

From her vantage point above everyone's head, Cassie looked down at the place where Emma had been standing. The basket was on the ground but Emma was no longer there, nor was Alfred. Cassie's face wore a troubled frown as she opened the door and walked into the house.

Immediately the frown vanished. There was a lovely smell coming from the kitchen that hadn't been there early this morning when she'd made Pa a breakfast, all cold except for coffee reheated over the last dying embers in the stove. Hardly pausing for a reassuring glance at the blue sugar bowl when she reached the kitchen, Cassie ran over to the table. There on the red-checked cover lay a roast chicken, still warm from Mrs. Doctor's oven, a cold boiled ham, two pies, and an orange sponge cake that Cassie was certain contained nine eggs. With each offering there was a note in a different handwriting wishing them a happy journey; other notes told of more food to come. Almost every woman in Katonah had either sent or promised something. She wouldn't need to cook a single thing until the house was on the ground again.

Cassie's heart swelled until she felt all crowded inside; then she flew back to the porch and leaned out over the railing.

"Pa, oh, Pa, come up and see! It's a surprise. A wonderful surprise!"

After they had finished eating, Cassie went to the well for a bucket of water, which she hoisted up to the house on a pulley that Pa had attached to a porch pillar. This was the way they would get whatever water they needed until they were too far from their own well to carry. After that they would have to borrow from wells along the way.

When she had washed and dried the dishes, Cassie took the damp towel out on the porch to hang on the line Pa had put up for her. It was where she'd have to hang all their laundry, underclothes and all, until they had a yard of their own once more.

Towel still in hand, she looked down at the men and boys who had started work again. Ollie and Joe and Ralph were working with a group carrying timbers from the back of the house to the front; Jabez and Caleb were helping Pa build the cribbing that would make the new tracks level.

Pa had warned her not to expect the whole journey to go as smoothly as it had begun. He said that was too much to hope and that there was chance of accident any time, but watching the care with which he put each piece of wood in place, Cassie was confident. There would be no accident. To be sure, living in a house on the move would have its inconveniences, but mostly it was going to be simply elegant fun.

Sleigh bells jingled, snow flew out from beneath swift hoofs, and a moment later the judge reined in his handsome bay colt with a lively flourish. Seth and Moses ran up to unhitch Prince from the cutter, and Cassie flapped her stiffening towel at the judge in greeting. He acknowledged the salute by touching his sealskin hat and then walked over to the house and stood below her.

"Cassie, child, come down a minute," he said. "The climb is too high for an old man like me."

Cassie vaulted over the porch railing and dropped to the ground. The judge waved a hand toward Jabez and Caleb. "Noah not here?"

"No, sir, he isn't." The conversation that she'd scarcely heeded earlier came back to her. "Caleb said Noah was afraid to come. He said the constable has been bothering him to remember something he's forgot."

Curiosity that she hadn't felt before stirred in Cassie. "Why should the constable be bothering Noah, do you suppose?"

The judge frowned. He seemed angry but it wasn't with her. "Because the constable's a—" He broke off and began again. "The unfortunate part is that Noah *can't* remember and neither can the others. Even Hattie isn't sure. Cassie, can you recall on which day of the week you helped the men cut the Dickinson Christmas tree?"

The question surprised Cassie and made her feel guilty. "Aunt Hattie asked me that, too, and I couldn't remember because I was all excited about plans to move the house. Later I did, though. I should have gone back and told her. It was Wednesday."

The judge nodded, looking as though her answer pleased him. "Hattie thought the same but she couldn't swear to it. Could you?"

"Why, yes. It was only a couple of minutes after the tree fell that I heard the Rocking Stone—then later when I got home Pa told me the City was going to take this land—then almost right away he had to leave to work the pump on 'Little Giant.' Is it important, sir?"

"Yes, Cassie, it is." His voice was grave. "Some folks in town would like to see Noah sent away. They think there's harm in him because he's simple."

"How awful of them!" Cassie cried in dismay. "Noah

is *good*—all the derelicts are good."

"*We* know that, child, and others do, too, but proving it might be hard. However, I still have hopes of persuading the folks who want him sent away to change their minds."

Suddenly he smiled and Cassie felt reassured. Noah wouldn't be sent away so long as the judge was on his side.

"We are ready now, Judge," Mr. Fowler called. He was standing beside the capstan and the judge's horse was hitched to the bar. "Can I drive Prince for you?"

"Don't talk about this, Cassie," the judge said in a low tone. "Not to anyone unless I say so." Then he raised his voice to a jovial shout.

"No, sir! You *can't* drive Prince. No one drives that colt but me!"

13

Dreadful News

It was Wednesday morning and just beginning to get light. Cassie opened her eyes and then closed them again, giving herself a few more minutes of warmth beneath the covers. In the four days she'd been living in a house on the move, there had been plenty of the fun she'd anticipated, but among the expected inconveniences she hadn't counted on the wicked cold. It crept under the house, standing so high off the ground, and slipped up between the floor boards in icy gusts that rippled the rugs and nearly froze her feet, no matter how many pairs of woolen stockings she wore. Pa couldn't keep fires going long enough to heat the house through. Every afternoon as soon as moving stopped, he built fires but they had to let them die down before moving started again in the morning.

Cassie counted to ten slowly. When she reached ten she threw back the covers and jumped out of bed before she could lose courage. Then, shivering into her clothes, outside jacket and all, she ran downstairs to set last night's coffee to warm over the few live coals that still glowed in the kitchen range.

Outside, the sky turned from dark gray to pearl with a few rosy streaks. Cassie went to the window above the sink and looked out with the feeling of strangeness she experienced every morning. From this same window for nearly three years, she had seen Pa's blacksmith shop. Now what she saw was the railroad tracks and beyond them a narrow strip of flat, snow-covered fields, abruptly terminated by sheer cliffs. Tomorrow the house would be right in the middle of the nearest field. Pa was planning to move it across the tracks between the 12:20 train north and the 2:15 south.

This was still the plan when Cassie set off for school after breakfast, but at the last minute the plan had to be changed. Just as Pa had started moving timbers after the 12:20 passed, word had come that Mrs. Doctor needed her mare in a hurry because the Wilcox baby up near Mt. Holly had decided to arrive a week early. So Queenie had to be unhitched from the capstan and another horse found to take her place. That had delayed the crossing until the next long interval between trains, late in the afternoon. School was out by then.

Running down the tracks, Cassie had been surprised

to see the house still on the west side of the railroad and nearly half the men in the village working. It was a race against time now, Mr. Prouty, the hotel owner, told her as she reached the scene of activity.

"Here, take hold of that end with Caleb," he said, lifting the other end of a cribbing timber himself.

For the next half hour Cassie helped lift and carry. The beams were short but solid, and each seemed heavier than the one before. Pa was building the cribbing across the rails slowly and deliberately: two pieces north and south and two pieces resting on them east and west, like a giant tic-tac-toe pattern, growing higher and higher.

"Better hurry there, Bates," Mr. Green urged. "Only a little over an hour left."

"I haven't time to hurry," Pa replied, testing the firmness of the beam he had just laid. "This has got to hold."

At last he was satisfied with the cribbing, and the long timbers were brought forward and laid on top. By that time even Old Bess, who had replaced Queenie at the capstan, appeared to share the tense feeling of the humans and was pawing the snow in unaccustomed impatience.

When finally Pa gave the signal to start, it seemed to Cassie that every single person in the crowd let out a sigh at the same time.

Only one set of timbers had to be traversed in order to cross the rails, but as Mr. Miller drove Bess around and around the capstan, watches were pulled out of pockets every minute or two and, as it grew darker, consulted by the flare of sulphur matches.

"Want Bess to move out faster?" Mr. Miller asked.

Pa looked at his own watch. "She's doing just fine, thanks. Just keep her steady."

Cassie was torn between trust in Pa's judgment and a desire for haste. She felt disloyal every time she cast a fearful glance up the tracks but she couldn't help doing it.

Inch by inch and foot by foot the house went forward. Cassie's arms ached from wanting to push. In the distance she heard a faint toot-toot. The crossing above Golden's Bridge? Or the one farther north? Her eyes strained into the distance, trying to see around curves.

When she looked back, the last inch of house had crossed over onto the set of timbers waiting on the other side. Cassie felt all weak and wobbly with relief but the next instant worry began again.

"Get that lumber off the tracks!" For the first time she heard hurry in Pa's voice.

Everyone rushed to carry the beams and cribbing to safety. Cassie looked at the big pile of lumber that was left and then put her ear down on the rails and listened. That way a person could hear a train coming before he could see it. There was a rumble in the rails all right and it was growing louder and louder. She listened only a moment and then she flung herself back into work. Only Pa and Mr. Creighton seemed sure that they'd make it in time.

Then at last it was over. The very last pieces of lumber were off the track and there was time to spare. Ten minutes later the train came thundering by, whistle blowing and searchlight streaming down the rails. The engineer leaned out of the cab to wave and the crowd let out a cheer that old Mrs. Blaney, who was deaf, claimed afterward to have heard clear up on Main Street.

When the house was at the end of the third set of timbers, work stopped and Pa asked everyone in for supper. There was plenty of food, and with fires built up it was soon warm enough to take off coats and mittens. It was while she was eating some of Mrs. Daniels' famous shoofly pie that Cassie heard Mr. Creighton say something that made her swell with pride. Mr. Creighton had been coming by once or twice a day ever since moving began; now he said he wouldn't be stopping any more.

"You don't need me," he told Pa. "You're a natural-born engineer and a fine work boss." He had gone on to say nice things about the heavy jacks Pa had invented and about the improvement for capstans, too. Cassie, listening, with a piece of pie in her mouth, had almost choked on a raisin.

Now that they were on the east side of the tracks, the worrisome time was over, anyway. Only flat land lay between the house and Mr. Daniels' potato field. By Friday, or Saturday at the latest, Pa expected to set it down on its new foundation.

Tomorrow morning there would be nearly a quarter mile of unbroken snow for Cassie to tramp through on the way to school but by the time school let out, the house would be closer; she might even be able to see Pa from the silk mill. She'd wave, but she wouldn't be coming home. She was to stay the night with Emma at the manse because there was to be an evening meeting about the contract for the new schoolhouse. Pa was going to the meeting and he wasn't willing for her to be alone, across the tracks, so far from the village.

Visiting Emma was always fun and now there was an added pleasure to look forward to. For the first time in nearly a week her toes would have a chance to thaw out completely.

There was a furnace in the manse and a real bathroom—one of the three indoor bathrooms Katonah boasted. After supper when Mr. Ferris had gone to the school meeting and the dishes were done, Mrs. Ferris gave Cassie permission to use all the hot water left in the tank for a bath. It was blissful to lie in hot water up to her chin in the big copper tub, and afterward it was blissful to jump into the big double bed in Emma's room under the eider-down quilt sprigged with pretty flowers.

When Mrs. Ferris came upstairs she turned down the lamps and kissed the girls good night. Then it was secret-telling time. Cassie wished she could tell about the people who wanted to send Noah away, but she couldn't because of her promise to the judge. Perhaps, though, Emma wouldn't have waited to listen anyway. As soon as her mother's door closed, she grabbed Cassie's hand and put it on the front of her ruffled challis nightgown, where a small hard object lay suspended from a ribbon.

"Cassie, feel!" she whispered.

In spite of the words she had heard Emma and Alfred exchange on the first day of moving, it was a shock to feel the ring. Cassie had wanted to think that the words had meant nothing; that Emma had grown tired of Alfred, as Josie believed.

"Oh, Emma," she said, "I hoped—I just hoped you didn't really like him any more."

Emma giggled. "I don't really. Not as much as Ralph, if he liked *me,* or even as much as George Tyler. But Alfred's exciting and they aren't. Can't you understand, Cassie?"

"No," Cassie said, wishing her voice didn't sound so stiff. "No, I can't."

"You will some day," Emma assured her. "It's a tingly feeling and sort of scary, too, the way I feel about Alfred. He wants to take me to a party over at Amawalk, at Gertie Perkins' house."

So that was what they'd been talking about!

"But you can't, Emma! No one's allowed to go to Gertie's house. Why, she's *fast!*" Gertie's father ran a saloon in part of his home and sometimes Gertie helped at the bar.

"Papa and Mama think so, too, but Alfred says she's as nice as can be." Emma sighed happily. "Maybe I won't go but maybe I will. I could walk the ledge outside my window until I came to the maple and then shinny down. Alfred will be waiting in one of his father's cutters. He has it all planned."

"You wouldn't!" Cassie was truly horrified now. She had to stop Emma. "It isn't only Gertie that's fast. Alfred is, too. He smokes cigarettes!"

"Of course he does." Emma gave a superior little laugh. "I know that. He let me try one once but I didn't like it."

Cassie came to a sudden decision. She'd have to tell Emma about the stealing. She drew a quick breath.

"All right then, but do you know where he *gets* his cigarettes? He bribes the little boys to steal them for him." As soon as it was said, Cassie wished it unsaid. Just as she'd feared all along, it only made Emma rush to Alfred's defense.

"That's a hateful thing for you to say, Cassie Bates. It's not true!"

"It is." Anyway it had been true.

"Did the little boys say so?"

"No." Cassie couldn't tell her who had said so. The

story would go right back to Alfred, and the derelicts were in enough trouble as it was.

"Then you're making it up!" Emma drew way over to her side of the bed, and Cassie to hers. Neither spoke again but neither slept.

Both girls heard Mr. Ferris when he returned. The door to the bedroom next to Emma's opened.

"How was the meeting, dear?" Mrs. Ferris asked. "Which contract are they taking?"

"Neither." Mr. Ferris sounded as though the heart had gone out of him. "I don't know how to tell you, Elizabeth."

"Tell me what, dear?"

"We are not going to rebuild."

"But why, Charles? The insurance was paid. Three thousand dollars. Isn't that enough?" Mrs. Ferris' voice was puzzled.

"We won't need a school. Katonah has been condemned."

There was a sharp indrawn breath on the other side of the thin partition.

Emma inched over toward the middle of the bed and her hand sought Cassie's. "Oh, Cassie, what does he *mean?"*

Mrs. Ferris' voice rose high in dismay. "But the survey showed that only the land on the river would be flooded. It *did,* Charles. There must be some mistake!"

Of course there was a mistake, Cassie whispered to Emma. She had pored over the map in Mr. Daniels' office until she knew every curve of the water line as Mr. Creighton had drawn it.

"This has nothing to do with the survey, or with the Aqueduct Commission either," Mr. Ferris answered his wife. "Do you remember that man from the Department of Public Works who was in town last week?"

"Yes?"

"Well it seems he was here to take samples of water from our streams and rivers. A report came out today. It says our sewage is seeping into the Cross and Croton rivers, right now. The sources of our sewage will be even closer to them after the new dam is finished and the water level rises. The report claims bacteria will be carried all the way down to the Croton Reservoir and pollute New York City's water supply."

Mr. Ferris gave a short, bitter laugh. "Water's been healthy enough for us all these years, but the City's got its wind up. It wants all our land vacated clear to the tracks. Not just the part that will be flooded."

"Oh, Charles, no!"

Cassie and Emma clung together, frightened but still not quite believing.

"Yes, my dear." Mr. Ferris sounded as though he

were struggling to subdue a fierce and unholy anger. "The Department of Public Works has ordered us out of our homes. Out of our beautiful churches, too."

Emma's grip tightened until Cassie's hand felt numb. "Oh, Cassie, what will happen to us? What will we *do?*"

In the next room Emma's mother must have asked the same question because Mr. Ferris answered it. "We must pray, my dear, pray to accept whatever comes with fortitude."

Hardly aware of what they were doing, Emma and Cassie slipped out of bed and down to their knees on the floor.

"We must pray, too," Emma whispered.

While Mr. Ferris' words of prayer came to them through the wall, Cassie put in a silent plea, all her own.

"Please don't make us accept, God. Please don't make us. Send down a thunderbolt or—or something."

14

Ollie Speaks His Mind

By the time school opened the next morning, every child in Katonah had heard the dreadful news.

"Oh, Cassie, I just can't believe it!" Josie cried when they had taken their seats. "It's like in that poem *Evangeline* that Mr. Tyler read out loud, where everyone had to leave Acadia. Only it's happening to us. It's us who are going to be separated forever!"

"The City has no right to take land it isn't going to flood!" Ollie protested angrily. "I'll lay an axe on anyone who tries to touch our house!"

Cassie twisted around and looked at his defiant red face and belligerently thrust-out jaw. She knew he wouldn't really dare take an axe to anyone but his threat made her feel better somehow.

Mr. Tyler rapped on his desk for order and when the room was quiet, he stood up. His eyes, usually so stern behind his thick lenses, went from row to row, from face to face, lingering a moment on each as though he loved them all. Then he bowed his head.

"O Lord, give us strength to accept thy will," he prayed.

Cassie stiffened. Not Mr. Tyler too! Were all the grownups going to accept this terrible thing as God's will?

Mr. Tyler raised his head and when he spoke, it was as though he were speaking to equals.

"None of us will find it easy to keep our minds on study today," he said, "but we must try. It is now doubly important that we work our hardest during the rest of this term. The eighth grade will be finishing school in June; the seventh will be entering new schools next fall. I, too, will be in a new school. Wherever I may be, I want to feel proud of the education that my Katonah pupils will carry with them."

He paused to clear his throat and then concluded, "The City will have taken our school, but remember, all of you, that it can never take away what you have learned in it."

Across the aisle Cassie could see Emma and Estelle weeping silently. Josie threw open the top of their desk and dabbed at her eyes with a handkerchief. Cassie's throat felt so sore she could scarcely bear it. The silence that followed Mr. Tyler's words was unbearable, too. It was a relief to everyone when over their heads the big looms of the silk mill all started up at once with a bang-crash that shook the building.

Mr. Tyler had to shout to make himself heard.

"We will now proceed with our lessons. The seventh grade will please take out their geographies."

At recess time, the snow forts stood deserted and not a snowball was let fly. All over the play yard, boys and girls gathered in small desolate groups to compare what their parents had told them. Some families had already made tentative plans for the future.

"Pa figures on moving to Peekskill on account of Uncle Eben living there. He figures Uncle Eben will help him get started in business again."

"Ma's cousin married a man over in Jersey; I guess we will go live in Hackensack to be near them. I just know I'll hate Hackensack!"

In other families there were no plans—only panic because plans would have to be made.

"My folks don't know *what* to do. Ma is near crazy with worry."

Listening, Cassie wondered miserably what was to become of her. Since the blow had fallen on Katonah, she hadn't even seen Pa. Morning prayers at the manse had stretched on and on as Mr. Ferris prayed for every family in the village. When he finished, there was no time to run home before school as she'd intended. As it was, she and Emma had been the very last ones into the building.

"Where are *you* going, Cassie?" Estelle Whitlock asked.

Pa would have to start looking again for a place to rent. And it wasn't fair when he'd worked so hard to move their house!

Cassie was about to reply that she didn't know where they'd move when Alfred spoke up.

"*She* doesn't have to go anywhere. *Her* house is safe on this side of the tracks. The City isn't taking this side. Didn't you all know?"

Cassie's heart gave a tremendous leap. When Mr. Ferris had explained that the village would have to be vacated, she'd assumed he'd meant both sides of the tracks. Or perhaps he hadn't known the east side was to be spared, because he'd prayed for Pa and her, too. She looked down the fields at her house. So it wouldn't have to be destroyed! She and Pa could still live in it! For a moment she knew a dizzying, unthinking happiness until Alfred's voice cut through it.

"Look at her! So long as she's safe, she don't care what happens to the rest of us." There was contempt in his voice, as though for a traitor.

Cassie couldn't face the eyes turned toward her but she could feel their resentment boring into her until her happiness was riddled with holes. She understood the resentment; she'd had to fight against it in herself when the river land had been condemned and the rest of the village was thought safe.

It wasn't entirely fair, though. It was true that for a moment she'd thought only of her house but she did care what happened to the others. Of course she did. She longed to tell them so, but she stood frozen and incapable of saying a single word.

"Ralph Creighton should be real proud of his pa," Alfred went on bitterly. "After school I'm going to maul Ralph up so good that his pa will wish he'd never heard of Katonah."

"No, you're not," Joe told him. "His pa had nothing to do with this. If you set on Ralph, you'll have to fight me, too."

After Alfred turned away, Joe spoke again. "I'm real glad your house will be safe, Cassie." Incredibly his voice sounded friendly toward her.

"So am I, Cassie. Oh, so am I!" Josie cried.

Then Cassie could look at them again. Alfred had gone to join Emma on the other side of the yard, but the others were still there and they all seemed as glad for her as Joe and Josie. Their moment of resentment had passed as quickly as her own moment of unthinking selfishness.

She swallowed a big hard lump. "I *do* care what

happens to you. I do—I do! I wish you all could stay. I wish you all could come live with me and Pa!"

"I wish so, too," Josie said wistfully. "Seems as though I'll just about die when I have to leave Katonah. I don't want to go to a new school. I don't want to make new friends. I want the ones I have right here."

"I feel the same," Estelle agreed. "I won't belong anywhere else."

"Well, *I'm staying!*" Ollie announced, kicking at a lump of frozen snow with the copper toe of his boot. "And my folks are, too."

Cassie hadn't let herself dare hope that Katonah could be saved except by an unlikely miracle. All that Mr. Ferris and Mr. Tyler had asked, even of God, was strength to accept the situation. Now suddenly it was as though one of those new electric bulbs had been lit up inside her. Perhaps some of the older people *weren't* accepting.

"Oh, Ollie, I thought all the grownups had given in! I didn't know your folks—"

"They don't know it yet," he interrupted, glowering fiercely. "They aim to leave but I ain't going to let them. Like I said before, I'll lay an axe to any City fellow who tries to touch our house."

The light went out. Ollie was just boasting again. A moment later he abandoned bravado for aggrieved complaint.

"Pa and Ma *ought* to stay." His voice started gruff and then rose high and cracked. "So should all the other grownups. They shouldn't just walk out because the City says 'Vamoose'!"

Ollie's words brought into the open the sense of betrayal that had lain close under the surface in the heart of almost every Katonah child.

"Sure they should stay!" Another boy backed him up hotly. "They should stand and give the City fellows *what for.* If they did, they could send them packing in less time than it takes to say 'Jack Robinson.' "

"Seems like they should be ashamed." Estelle Whitlock scowled. There was a loud chorus of agreement.

It was what Cassie had been feeling all morning but she knew she couldn't have come right out against Pa like that if he'd been among the parents abandoning their homes. She would have kept still like Joe and Josie but she would have felt ashamed for him inside.

"They oughtn't to talk so, even if it's true," Josie said in a low, miserable voice.

"Maybe it's not true. Maybe—" Joe began.

"Maybe what, Joe?" Emma had crossed the yard to join them.

"Maybe . . ." Suddenly he shrugged. "I don't know. I was asleep when Pa got back last night and he was gone when I woke up. Ma wasn't at the meeting. She couldn't tell me much. I guess I don't know any more than the other kids."

Recess ended and the three girls and Joe walked back toward the silk mill together. At the door they stopped before going in.

"So long as you're here, Cassie, we can all come back and visit," Josie said. "The woods will be the same. We can still play on the Rocking Stone."

"I'll come often," Emma promised.

"So will I," Joe said.

But they all knew it might not be possible; that they might be too widely separated.

Cassie gulped. Perhaps Joe and Emma and Josie would never play on the Rocking Stone again after leaving Katonah. Perhaps in their new homes they wouldn't have any woods, or any water to row and skate on.

She reached for Josie's right hand and Emma's left and squeezed them tight. It was safer than trying to speak.

At lunch hour Cassie ran home. As she neared the house, she could see that there was no one outside and that smoke was coming from the chimney. Perhaps everyone felt too bad to help with the moving today, but Pa would be there. He'd know she needed him. She found him sitting at the kitchen table, his face sad and old-looking.

"I thought you'd come, Cassie. I have two horses waiting to be shod but I had to be here if you came."

"Yes, Pa. I knew you'd be here. Oh, Pa, isn't there any way to save Katonah? If the people put up a fight—if they didn't just give in?"

He shook his head. "Wouldn't do any good, honey. State law gives the City the right to take as much land as they need to insure pure water. Guess the State Militia would put people off if they didn't go peaceful like."

"It isn't fair! Oh, Pa, I feel so sorry for Josie and Emma and all the others who have to move away!"

Pa looked at her as though she'd said something that hurt him, something he hadn't expected. He gave a sigh that seemed to come right up from his boots.

"I wish you had already thought it out, Cassie." He shook his head. "I wish I didn't have to tell you."

"Tell me what, Pa? The City isn't going to take this side of the tracks. Didn't you know?"

"I know, Cassie."

"What is it then, Pa? What is it?"

"There are only three buildings on this side of the tracks." He paused, waiting for her to understand, to say something that showed she understood. Then he went on, slowly, as though each word was misery to speak. "When the rest of the village goes, there will be no horses."

Cassie felt stunned. As that passed, shame took its place. "I should have known, Pa. You shouldn't have had to say it."

"Cassie, it ain't right that you should have to move again. I'd promised myself it wouldn't happen."

"I know, Pa, but don't feel so bad. I guess I don't mind much." Wanting to comfort him, Cassie suddenly knew her words were true.

"Not mind, Cassie?"

"No. When the others came to leave, I guess I wouldn't want to stay."

Pa looked, not happy, but as though the heaviest part of a weight had been lifted.

"We won't move the house any farther, honey, but I can make it tight against the cold with boards. Then, perhaps, when the people begin to move I can find a shop some place near at least one of your friends."

"That would be lovely, Pa." She leaned over and kissed the top of his head. "I'd like that." But she knew it mightn't work out so he could.

Faintly she could hear the big cowbell that Mr. Tyler had used since the fire, ringing in the distance.

"I have to go now." Still she didn't move. "Pa, do *you* think it's God's will for everyone to be separated?"

"No, honey, I don't. I think He'd like us all to stay together."

"So do I, Pa, oh, so do I! I prayed last night that God would send a thunderbolt to keep it from happening. Was that wrong?"

Pa gave a wintry-looking smile. "Well now, Cassie, I'm not just sure a thunderbolt would be the best way. Perhaps God could think of a better way Himself. Perhaps He'd like to do His own thinking."

Suddenly Pa began to chortle. "Cassie, you certainly

do beat the Dutch. As long as I have you, I'll do fine anywhere."

"The same goes for me, Pa." But Cassie knew this wasn't true. Wherever she went she'd ache and ache for Josie and Emma.

15

Noah in Danger

"If only we three could move to the same place, it wouldn't be so awful," Josie said.

"No, it wouldn't," Emma agreed, "but Papa can't even choose where we will go. He has to be *called* somewhere by a church that needs a minister."

The three girls were on their way to Emma's house after school and Cassie had just told them what Pa had said about moving near at least one of her friends. It wasn't anything she could count on but she'd wanted to talk about it. They were walking along River Road when Joe caught up with them.

"Hey, Cassie, have you forgotten what day it is?"

"Day?" She looked at him blankly. Of course she knew what day it was. She'd never forget this day—the one after the school meeting where the grownups had learned Katonah must be vacated.

"It's Thursday. You can't just walk off. You've got

to work on the paper," he told her.

Cassie sighed. Joe was right. She always worked Thursdays and Fridays, and now Mr. Daniels was short-handed again and needed her more than usual. She couldn't just walk off. Reluctantly she turned away from the girls and went back up Main Street with Joe.

They found Mr. Daniels hunched over his desk in the back office. His thinning hair was rumpled and he was frowning at the words he had just written. Impatiently, he crossed them out and began again, pencil squeaking rapidly across the page. Scribbled sheets of paper filled the wire basket on the desk top and lay scattered about on the floor by his feet. Cassie stooped to pick one up. It read: COMMISSIONER OF PUBLIC WORKS ORDERS KATONAH OFF THE MAP; and it was underlined twice to show it was intended for a headline.

"Leave it be, Cassie," Mr. Daniels said, looking up briefly. "Run downstairs, both of you, and start setting up the short pieces I laid out on the shelf under the type cabinet. Do the best you can without bothering me; I haven't finished my editorial yet."

Downstairs, Joe lit the lamps and divided the sheaf of notes on the shelf, giving half to Cassie. She wasn't as quick as he at setting type but she'd learned to be accurate enough so that each letter no longer needed concentration. First she set the items which would appear under the heading *Katonah Jottings.*

The Ladies of the Methodist Church will hold a rummage sale on Friday next, the proceeds to go toward a new carpet. . . .

Mrs. Hazleton plans to visit her mother in Croton Falls next week. . . .

The gramophone concert given at Prouty's Hotel on Saturday evening was well attended. . . .

It seemed incredible to Cassie that such things still mattered enough to print. When she started in on the advertisements, they, too, seemed to belong to some time long past. Who, now, could possibly care that the Great American Tea Company was seeking a "Katonah Club Representative to introduce their celebrated goods"?

Around five o'clock Joe had finished his share of the work and Cassie was clamping the lines she had just set in a frame, when Mr. Daniels came down the stairs. He looked tired and he kept stretching his neck to get the kinks out of it.

"I have part of a column still to fill on the extra page I'm running," he said. "Thought I might put in something about how the young folks feel. What about the boys at school, Joe?"

"You really want to know?" Joe asked, shuffling a stack of notes together.

"I'm asking, son."

"Well then." Joe looked uncomfortable. "Well then, they're boiling mad. Mad at the City and mad at their folks for giving in to the City without a fight. I guess we all think our folks can do about anything they set their minds to, and here they've gone and quit without even trying."

"You feel that way, Joe?"

"I'm not mad at you, Pa, if that's what you mean, but it would make me feel a whole lot better if you did something."

"I'd feel a lot better myself if there was something I could do," Mr. Daniels said grimly. "Only it's no use fighting the City. State law is on their side. City politicians got a bill shoved through last session. If I'd been home at breakfast time instead of at the judge's house, I would have told you. I'm printing the law, just as it stands in the judge's law book. If the boys bother to read it, maybe they will think better of their parents."

He turned to Cassie. "What was the talk among the girls, Cassie? They mad at their folks, too?"

Cassie thought back. "I only heard one girl say so. Mostly the talk was about being split up, having to make new friends and all. Josie said it was like the poem *Evangeline,* only happening to us."

"Acadia, eh?" Mr. Daniels looked thoughtful. "Not a bad comparison, that."

"If only some of us could move to the same places, like Pa promised me, we wouldn't feel so terrible." Again Cassie repeated Pa's promise to move near at least one of her friends, then added realistically, "But most likely he won't be able to. He'll have to go some place where people *need* a blacksmith, just like Mr. Ferris will have to go where they need a minister."

"I guess it's the same for all of us, Cassie," Mr. Daniels said wearily. "I'll have to find a town where there is no paper or where an editor is ready to sell out. Mr. Miller will have to settle where another market is needed, and Mr. Arnold where there is a need for good shoes."

He sighed. "Well, you had best be getting along now. Joe, tell your ma I won't be back for supper. Ask her to fix something you can bring down to me."

"I'll walk you home first, if you'd like, Cassie," Joe offered.

Cassie refused and a moment later regretted it. It would be dark on the other side of the tracks, once she passed the lights of the silk mill. Snowy, too, she realized as she opened the outside door of the office. Large white flakes were whirling around the street lamp on the corner and two inches of new snow had built up on the ground while she'd been working inside. She was about to turn back and accept Joe's offer when the judge drove up and stopped in front of the building.

"Hop in, Cassie, your father told me where to find you."

Prince was feeling fresh and dancing up and down. Cassie had to make a quick jump into the cutter. Then, as she settled under the buffalo robe, the judge gave the colt his head and he leaped forward. After that he never seemed to set hoof to the ground. They flew along, bells jangling wildly and snow dashing against their faces. Cassie clung to the side of the seat as they careened around corners. She had not even asked where they were going or why, when they drew up at the Dickinson House. Jabez came out to take Prince to the stable and the judge handed Cassie down and led her into the house.

Aunt Hattie was sitting alone in front of the coal grate in the back parlor. She gave Cassie a smile but she looked worried and distressed.

"We need your help, child," the judge said when they had removed their coats and hung them up.

Help? *She* help, when none of the grownups could do anything to save Katonah? Cassie looked at them inquiringly. But in a moment it turned out they wanted her for something quite different.

"It's about Noah," the judge told her. "He's in a peck of trouble. He's being accused of setting the fire that ignited the school, and the insurance company is bringing suit. I aim to defend him but it won't be easy.

Other side has a real good lawyer, too. Smart young fellow from White Plains."

Cassie sat down suddenly on the hassock by Aunt Hattie's feet. She felt a little dizzy. She remembered the judge talking to her about Noah, of course, but it seemed a lifetime ago, as did everything else that had happened before Katonah had been ordered to vacate.

Aunt Hattie leaned forward and put a hand on her hair. "Mrs. Blaney is going to be a witness. She is willing to swear Noah was in the shed where the fire started; that she saw him come out just a few minutes before it burst into flames."

"Oh no!" Cassie's denial was instinctive. "Anyway, who would believe her? Everyone knows she doesn't see much better than she hears."

"Those who want to believe her, do," the judge said dryly, "and that includes Henry Meech, who owns 80 per cent of the Mutual Company that insured the school building."

He took a cigar out of the case in his vest pocket and bit the end off it. "A jury is likely to believe her, too. The pesky thing is that Noah *was* back of that shed sometime during the day. His tracks were in the snow. They weren't trampled out like those around the school."

With a small pair of tongs Aunt Hattie lifted a coal that had fallen out onto the hearth. "You see, Cassie, the constable drew the tracks out on paper at the time, but he could never match them up until I sent Noah around with a dress pattern that his wife wanted last week. It was muddy on the walk and Noah made the same tracks right through the constable's kitchen."

"But the tracks behind the shed could have been made any time after it stopped snowing on the day of the fire," Cassie protested. "It stopped before noon. I know because Pa asked me to shovel our walk before I came up here to help you with cookies."

Aunt Hattie nodded. "If only Noah could have remembered *when* he was back of the shed, the constable might have believed him. But he couldn't; he said he wasn't there at all. That looked bad."

"Noah will make a very poor witness." The judge looked grave. "He's bound to get scared and mixed up. The jury will take Mrs. Blaney's word rather than his."

"Oh dear, what will happen then?" Cassie asked unhappily.

"Well, for one thing, the court is likely to make Noah pay damages," the judge told her. "Meech's company is asking three thousand dollars—that's what they had to pay out when the school burned."

"Three thousand dollars!" Cassie exclaimed. "But Noah doesn't have any money!"

"Yes he does, Cassie," Aunt Hattie spoke quietly,

"and Mr. Meech knows it. Ten years ago when Noah's niece died, he inherited thirty-two hundred dollars, which the judge has been handling for him. The interest hasn't always paid for Noah's expenses, but the judge and I put up the extra. None of the principal has ever been touched. He still has it all."

"And it isn't just the money." The judge drew savagely on his cigar. "Some people have been saying for years that Noah should be in an asylum. Ever since talk started about the possibility of him setting the fire they've been at it again. Unless we can get an airtight alibi for him, they may win out."

The thought of Noah locked up in an asylum was dreadful. It mustn't happen. But what could *she* do? Then she began to understand. Alibi, the judge had said.

"Is that how you want me to help?" she asked. "Do you want me to say I was with him?"

"Only if you can say so truthfully, but that is what we hope you can do. That is why we brought you here," the judge said. "*Were* you with Noah at five o'clock on the afternoon of the fire?"

Both the judge and Aunt Hattie were looking at her expectantly. Five o'clock. It had been almost dark when she and Josie and Ollie and Joe left the derelicts in the woods and started back to the Triangle. But how could she swear to the exact time?

"I don't know," she faltered, miserable because she couldn't help.

"Try to think, child."

Cassie tried to think of something, anything that would set the time. The judge and Aunt Hattie talked in low tones so as not to disturb her.

Jabez came into the room and she glanced up. He was carrying a shoe.

"Hattie, I need some more of that waxed thread," he said. "Noah is always busting this toe open. Wish the constable would give him back his good shoes—the ones I found in the dump."

"So do I, Jabez." She rose and went to her sewing basket. "But he says he has to keep them for the trial. They will be part of the evidence."

Cassie's eyes were still on Jabez. The shoe in his hand was gaping at the toe just the way it had gaped open while they were cutting the Christmas tree.

Five o'clock. She dug her fingernails into her palms and tried to concentrate on time again, but something began nibbling at the edge of her consciousness that hadn't to do with time.

Aunt Hattie found the thread for Jabez and he went back into the kitchen. The nibbling continued. It bothered Cassie so she had to ask.

"Aunt Hattie, why did the constable take the other

shoes? Noah was wearing the ones Jabez is mending on the afternoon of the fire."

"What!" The judge's voice sounded like an explosion. "Do you know what you are saying, child?"

"Yes, sir. The constable took the wrong shoes. He should give them back."

"Cassie, are you quite sure?" Aunt Hattie's voice was trembling.

"She will have to see the others, Hattie; she may be mistaken."

Five minutes later, Cassie and the judge were standing in the constable's cold and cheerless parlor.

"Of course, Your Honor, if you say so. No harm in showing them to her." The constable went upstairs and brought back a pair of shoes which he placed in Cassie's hands.

"Look at them very carefully, child," the judge admonished. "There must be no mistake."

Cassie didn't need a second look to know she had not been mistaken, but because the judge seemed so concerned, she turned them this way and that; even upside down. Suddenly she stiffened and her breath came short.

"Sir, Noah couldn't possibly have been wearing these shoes on the afternoon of the fire. Alfred Meech was wearing them." She ran her fingers along the nails in

the half sole, and pointed to one different from the others. "Josie and I drew pictures in our notebooks but I would have remembered anyway."

She told about the Vigilante Society and about the pow-wows where Alfred taught the little boys to smoke, and about the signal on the Rocking Stone.

"Because we'd already drawn them, Josie and I both knew they were Alfred's prints that we saw on the Rocking Stone the afternoon of the fire. Besides, Noah *was* with us at five o'clock. I've just remembered. The 5:05

whistled right after we said good-by to the derelicts. Josie will remember, too, and so will Joe and Ollie.

The judge and the constable looked at each other.

"Do you still have that notebook you drew in?" the constable asked.

Cassie nodded. "In my bureau drawer."

"Well," said the judge softly and in deep satisfaction. "Looks as though there's not much of a case against Noah. Guess there won't even be a trial when I tell all this to Henry Meech."

16

Village Meeting

The constable took Cassie home and waited while she ran upstairs for her Vigilante notebook. He told Pa why it was needed but asked both of them not to talk about it until after the judge had seen Mr. Meech.

It was hard for Cassie to keep still at school the next day, especially when Alfred was sent for in the middle of the morning, but she bit her tongue every time she was tempted to say something.

After school, all the while she was working on the newspaper, she kept wondering and worrying about what was happening. Then, late in the afternoon, Mr. Daniels came over to the bench where she and Joe were folding papers and said the judge was in the back office and wanted to speak to her.

Cassie took the stairs at a rush, hoping everything had turned out all right but half scared that it hadn't. The moment she got a full look at the judge, though, she knew that Noah was safe. The judge was standing by the map of the water level tacked onto the office wall, but when he heard her come into the room he turned and smiled in a way that showed he was satisfied. Then he began telling what had happened.

He and the constable had gone to see Mr. Meech together, taking with them the shoes and the drawings the constable and Cassie had made. The constable had also brought a statement by Mrs. Blaney, admitting that if she hadn't heard talk of the prints in the snow being Noah's, she wouldn't ever have been willing to swear it was he she'd seen leaving the shed at five o'clock on the afternoon of the fire. She had changed her mind about swearing it in court, now that she knew Noah had an alibi for that time.

"There won't be any trial, Cassie." The judge stopped and lit a cigar.

"But what about Alfred?" Cassie was afraid he had finished. It wasn't only about Noah she was thinking now, but Emma. The judge hadn't yet said anything that would prove to Emma—

"Well, that young man isn't too happy at the moment," the judge told her, going on. Alfred, it seemed, hadn't been able to deny the shoes had once been his, but he'd insisted at first that he'd discarded them in the dump several days before the fire. He insisted, too, that he hadn't left home all that afternoon but he couldn't stick with that story; not when the judge had suggested sending for Josie's little brothers. It had all come out then, how Alfred and the group of younger boys had been using the shed for pow-wows ever since Jabez had discovered them smoking in the cave.

"They were smoking there on the afternoon of the fire, but Alfred swore none of them knew they had started it until afterward."

The judge blew a smoke ring and watched it drift up toward the ceiling. "I'm willing to believe him on that. Alfred let the little boys in and out through a door facing the school, while he used an opening at the back. That's why Mrs. Blaney didn't see them, too."

"Did he tell about where they *got* the cigarettes?" This was what Emma had refused to believe two nights ago.

The judge nodded. "Yes, he confessed that, too."

Cassie felt a warm and happy satisfaction. Emma would have to believe now. Alfred wouldn't be able to spoil another minute of the time they had left in Katonah. She was thinking of this and only half paying attention when the judge began talking about Noah again.

"After I left the Meeches, I went up to the Dickinson House," he said. "When I told Noah that he didn't have to worry any more about trying to remember, that you had remembered for him and the constable wouldn't bother him again, he was so happy that he just sat there bawling for a while. Then he asked me if he had any money. He keeps forgetting. When I told him yes, he said he wanted you to have it all. I finally agreed to let him give you a hundred dollars."

"But he mustn't. I can't take it," Cassie protested, coming suddenly back to full attention. "It wouldn't be right to take money just for speaking the truth to help a friend."

"No, it wouldn't, Cassie," the judge agreed. "Not in the general run of things, but Noah doesn't think the way you and I do. He may not understand. I'm afraid it will hurt him badly if you refuse."

Cassie didn't want to hurt Noah; she couldn't even bear imagining it. But she couldn't accept a reward for speaking out either.

"Maybe," she spoke slowly because she was trying to think it out, "maybe he won't be hurt if I tell him how much I love him and promise he'll be the very first friend I'll ask for help the next time *I* need it."

And so it was left that Cassie would go and see Noah the next morning.

While they had been talking, the big press had been slap-banging and hissing under their feet. Pulling on his gloves, preparing to leave, the judge made a gesture toward the floor.

"A shame it's too late for one more item in the social news," he said, eyes twinkling. "Young Mr. Alfred Meech is leaving tonight for military school in Pennsylvania."

"Good riddance!" Cassie exclaimed. The next moment, though, she asked with a worried frown, "But what about the little boys? I hope nothing too bad will happen to them."

"Nothing more, anyway." The judge smiled. "Their fathers attended to them in their respective woodsheds as soon as school let out this afternoon."

By the next day everyone knew what had happened. Cassie expected Emma to find excuses for Alfred at first and be grief-stricken by his sudden departure, but she was mistaken.

"I'll miss him but I guess I'm really glad he's gone," Emma said seriously. "If he'd stayed, I'd have sneaked out to Gertie's party as sure as anything and done other exciting wrong things, too, but I would have hated myself for deceiving Mama and Papa."

The rest of the young people were frankly delighted by Alfred's comeuppance. Then in a day or two they forgot him except when they happened to notice his empty seat in the classroom.

They had more important things to think about. Under the headline, KATONAH A MODERN DAY ACADIA, Mr. Daniels had managed to put into words the children's feelings about being separated. Reading how the children felt, the older people realized they felt the same way, and were now making efforts to move in groups of two or more families instead of singly. But, as Mr. Daniels had foreseen, it wasn't going to be easy. The City wanted them off the land in six months and that didn't give much time to look around.

Newspapers from other areas were sent for, letters were written and maps were studied, and nothing much came out of it all.

Every man who owned a horse drove some neighbor to places they thought might suit, and Meech's horses and his big sleighs were at a premium. The judge and Prince seemed always on the road. Sometimes they had Mr. Fowler in the cutter, sometimes Mr. Hoyt or Mr. Prouty. More than once, Mr. Creighton was the judge's companion.

Several weeks passed and snow gave way to mud. Both wheels and spirits bogged down in it.

"I guess there's not much sense in hoping any more,"

Josie sighed at recess one day late in March. "Pa says he's got to find a place for us, even if we never see a single Katonah face again."

"My folks say the same." Ollie kicked at the one remaining lump of what had once been a snow fort. "And I ain't got any complaints. They've tried and tried so we'd have friends near."

"Papa has received an invitation to preach a sermon in Binghamton," Emma joined in bleakly. "If the elders like it, I guess we'll be moving there, just miles and miles from everyone."

Cassie felt as low in her mind as the others. Pa had done his share of driving around, too, and with no more success.

It was during this time of discouragement that the Village Improvement Society called a special meeting to be held in the big hall on the second floor of the hotel. Everyone knew it had something to do with the assessors coming to town again, and the values they were setting on property, but there were rumors of other business as well. Would the date of removal be extended? Was it possible that some part of the village farthest away from the water would be allowed to stand after all?

These guesses were enough to fill the hall with men and women and even the older children on the night of the meeting. Cassie and Pa sat next to the Ferrises.

Josie and her parents were in the row ahead.

Hardly anyone paid attention to the minutes of the previous meeting or the treasurer's report. They shuffled their feet impatiently as they waited for the main business to begin. No one, it seemed, was satisfied with what the City was willing to pay for their land, and later, when the judge warned them they had best accept the offers unless they were prepared to wait months or even years for their money, a storm of protest broke out.

Angry speeches were made. How did the City expect them to move without money? It wasn't fair treatment! After everyone who wanted to speak had been heard, the judge asked for the floor again.

"Neighbors," he said, "we've lived and done business with one another for a long time. We are used to each other's ways. We don't want to have to make new friends any more than the young people do. We don't want to join new churches and lodges. Well, the City says we've got to leave but it can't tell us we have to separate."

He paused and all over the hall whispering began. Was the judge in his dotage to say such a senseless thing? Hadn't they all been searching for weeks for new homes where they could be near even one other Katonah family?

Emma squeezed Cassie's hand. "What does he mean, Cassie? What do you suppose he means?"

"I don't know," Cassie whispered back. She was sure, though, that the judge wasn't just talking foolish.

He stood, thumbs in vest pockets, looking unperturbed while the whispering went on. When it stopped he spoke again.

"I see some of you think I've taken leave of my senses. Well, I haven't. I would have spoken out sooner except the time wasn't ripe for it. We had to get things sewed up first."

Mr. Prouty and Mr. Fowler were with Mr. Hoyt and the judge at the big table at the front of the room. They began to unroll a paper that lay on it. Necks were craned as everyone waited for the judge to continue.

He cleared his throat.

"That paper Mr. Prouty and Mr. Fowler have is a map of some land two miles down the track, empty fields now. Four of us took an option on it. Mr. Creighton assures us there's no chance there of the City claiming we'd pollute their water, and he helped us mark out streets and lots. If enough families make down payments on the lots in the next week, the land can be ours. We won't have to separate. We can all move together and make a new Katonah. What do you say, friends?"

After a moment of stunned silence, pandemonium broke loose. It wasn't possible to hear what anyone said in the din that followed, but there was no mistaking the answer to the judge's question. Men thumped each other on the back, women flung their arms around those sitting next to them, and boys drummed their boots on the floor. Josie hopped over the back of her seat to be with Cassie and Emma. None of the girls could say a word at first. It was enough just to hold tight to one another.

Then the crowd began to surge forward to the table. Cassie watched marks being made on the paper as men indicated their choices. Pa didn't go forward but it didn't worry her. From the way people talked when they came back from the table she knew the new Katonah was going to be larger than the present one. There would be—*there must be*—land for rent.

When all the grownups had looked, the young people had their turn. Studying the map, Cassie saw it included the land where she and Emma and Josie had gathered rushes that September day before school began. Across the railroad tracks and parallel to them was a road. Other roads ran west from this, up what Cassie knew was a gentle rise to the hills beyond. Lots were marked off and numbered.

Emma put three fingers on three lots; one already had *Manse* written on it. "Oh, I hope we can live on these three, right together," she said happily.

"Silly," Josie replied, but her voice was so happy,

too, that the teasing didn't count. "That spot is fine for the manse but a market has to be right on the main street. See, here it is." She pointed to a lot marked *Miller*, then turned to Cassie. "When is your Pa going to choose?"

Cassie looked back. Pa was still sitting as though glued to his chair. A little chill ran down her spine. Supposing there wasn't land for rent; suppose Pa knew it?

Mr. Prouty and Mr. Fowler had charge of the map but the judge was standing on one side answering questions. Emma and Josie went off to join some other young people standing against the wall but Cassie stayed behind, waiting for the judge to be free. She had to ask him, she had to know, before she spoke to Pa again.

At last he turned to her and she could ask, "Please, sir, will there be land to rent?"

The judge shook his head. "I'm afraid not, Cassie. Not now. Later some purchaser may be willing to rent a piece."

Later! But before then some other blacksmith, with money to buy, would have snatched up a lot and moved in. Even in this larger village there wouldn't be room for two blacksmiths.

The hall seemed to grow close and unbearably warm as self-pity almost stifled her. Cassie looked away, not wanting the judge to notice the tears in her eyes. Through a blur she saw that Aunt Hattie had come back to the table, bringing the derelicts with her. She was showing them the lot she had chosen. Why, even the derelicts would be part of the new village she would never live in, Cassie thought miserably. Even Jabez and Caleb and Noah were better off than she.

Noah! Cassie's heart gave a sudden thump. Then without giving herself time to change her mind, she went over to him.

"Noah," she said, her words tumbling out in a breathless rush, "Noah, I promised to ask you if I ever needed help. I need it now, bad. Will you lend me enough money for a down payment?"

The old man acted as though he didn't hear. "I shouldn't have asked," Cassie thought, but the next minute he beamed at her in surprised delight.

"Why, that's real kind of you, Cassie. I tried not to let on when you turned me down before but I was hurt in my heart. I figured you thought I wasn't good enough to take money from."

"It's just a loan," she tried to explain but in the old man's mind there was no difference.

When Cassie told the judge what she had done, he approved. "I am glad you did that, child. It will set up Noah's pride again," he said.

"But maybe I won't be able to pay him back for a long time." Cassie had begun to question the rightness of her act once more. "And the other payments. Perhaps we won't be able to put money by for them. Pa—" she gulped, "Pa is not a very saving man."

The judge smiled and turned her so she faced the rear of the hall. "Perhaps he's not, Cassie, but unless I'm much mistaken he's going to be a very earning man. Look."

Pa was no longer stuck to his chair. He was standing now, the center of a group of men, all talking to him. Mr. Miller was one of them. So were Mr. Arnold and Mr. Daniels. Mr. Ferris and several deacons of the church were there, too.

"Those of us who worked out this plan figured from the beginning on buying our homes back from the City and moving them with us." The judge nodded toward the group around Pa. "Looks as though others have hit on the same idea. After the way your father managed his own moving and invented those things that made it easier, he's the natural boss for the job. And I'll see he makes money on it, Cassie. I'll see that folks pay him right."

Cassie started back down the aisle, her heart so full that it hurt. In her mind she knew that she mustn't interrupt while Pa was talking business, but her feet didn't know. All by themselves they started running. Space opened for her in the crowd around Pa, and then Pa opened his arms. She flung herself into them.

"Pa, oh, Pa, we have a lot. Come pick it out quick!"

Pa looked puzzled, but excusing himself he followed Cassie back to the table at the front of the Hall. On the way she explained about Noah's loan.

"I couldn't let you take it, Cassie," he said, "except we can pay him back just as soon as we get the first houses to the new village." His eyes shone blue and proud. "Did you know folks are planning to take their houses with them? That they've asked me to do the moving?"

Cassie nodded. They were at the table now, looking down at the map. Pa put his finger on a lot south of the shops on the main street, just about the same distance as in the present village. The Millers were ten lots north, and the manse right back of them two blocks west.

"This suit you, honey?"

Cassie gave a blissful little sigh. "Oh, Pa, it's perfect."

Then, while Pa was making arrangements with Mr. Fowler, she looked around for Josie and Emma. She had to tell them. She had to tell them right away.

17

The Transplanting

By late August more than half the houses in Katonah were on the move to the new village. Though in the end the City had granted extra time to vacate, most people were eager to reach the new site and Pa wanted to get as many houses as possible back on foundations before winter set in.

Leaning against the porch railings of her own house, Cassie could see the river again, shimmering in the early morning light. Only it was from the bank opposite the Triangle that she was looking at it now. Pa had had to build a special bridge to bring the houses over on. Some folks had thought it couldn't be done, with the steep banks and all, but so far there hadn't been a single accident.

Across the river, Cassie could still make out the land on which their house and the blacksmith shop had stood. The little saplings that she'd helped plant in September marked the spot. They had grown some since winter but were still small enough to be dug up and transplanted later on.

Cassie thought about how she'd felt last winter, the night of Estelle's skating party, when she'd stood leaning against the porch railing just as she was doing now. Then she had wanted time to stand still and not a building nor a person to change. She'd wanted Emma and Josie and herself to stay the same ages forever so Emma couldn't grow away from them. When Pa told her all things must change, she hadn't wanted to believe him, but he'd been right. Inside, she felt different herself.

Along the dusty path beside the long wooden tracks on which Pa was moving six houses in a line, Mrs. Doctor came driving Queenie. She looked up and called to Cassie.

"Know where Prouty's Hotel is now?"

"Ahead about a quarter mile," Cassie told her. Mrs. Prouty had been hoping her seventh child would be the first baby born in the new Katonah, but Pa hadn't been able to get the hotel there in time.

As Mrs. Doctor hurried on, Joe and Ollie and Ralph came by. They were leading some horses up toward the capstans. All three boys had worked on the moving crew full time ever since school let out.

Ralph stopped below the porch. "Mother wants you

and Emma and Josie at eleven o'clock to practice the wedding music," he said.

"All right, I'll be there and I'll tell the others," Cassie promised. At noon Miss Williams was being married to Mr. Tyler's brother. *A Wedding on the Move*, she'd called it in her notes inviting people.

"Cassee-ee!" Josie leaned out of a window in the next house. "Cassie, come on over, I have something to tell you."

Cassie scrambled down off her own porch and up onto the Millers'.

"It's about Emma," Josie said. "You know what? She's not going to the Sunday School picnic with us next week. She's going with Ralph!" Josie sounded aggrieved but Cassie felt no answering resentment.

"It doesn't matter—not really," she told Josie. And it didn't. Emma was fourteen now, going on fifteen. She was growing up and nothing could stop that, but it didn't mean they were losing her. The three of them would always be best girl friends.

This year Emma would go to the picnic with Ralph and she and Josie would go together. Maybe it would be the same next year, but after that she and Josie would probably go to the picnic with boys, too.

Cassie knew Josie would hoot at this idea, so she didn't tell it to her. But she was glad time wasn't going to stand still for any of them. So many exciting things were just about to happen that she could hardly wait for each new day.

In a month they would be living in the new Katonah. The rosebush that had grown beside her house in the old village was already there, blooming in their new yard, waiting for them. The school was ready and waiting, too, built on the plans Mr. Tyler had shown them last winter.

All the streets that had been pencil marks on the map were real streets now. And along every one of them young trees were to be set out. Cassie had told Mr. Fowler that she'd work on the planting committee.

There would be plenty to do, settling the new Katonah and she, Cassie Bates, would help with it all. It would be her own village even more than the old one, because from the very first she'd be a part of it.

About the Author

Frances Duncombe lives only four miles from the old village of Katonah, the locale of her book. The background material for this novel is the result of research she did for a local history, *Katonah, the History of a New York Village and its People,* published in 1961.

Mrs. Duncombe is not a newcomer among juvenile fiction writers. Her first published books—in the 1940's—were for young people. Now, after an interim of years devoted to other kinds of writing, she has returned to her original field; the one she most enjoys.